COLD RE
A Sgt Major Cra
Book 1

By

Wendy Cartmell

TABLE OF CONTENTS

By Wendy Cartmell

Wendy Cartmell is a bestselling Amazon author, well known for her chilling crime thrillers. These include the Sgt Major Crane mysteries, Crane and Anderson police procedurals, the Emma Harrison mysteries and a cozy mystery series, set in Muddlebay. Further, a psychic detective series has been written, the first of which, Touching the Dead has been followed by six further books in the series. Finally, the haunted series is a collection of ghostly happenings in buildings or objects. Just click the covers to go to the book pages on Amazon.

Sgt Major Crane crime thrillers:

Crane and Anderson crime thrillers:

Emma Harrison mysteries

Supernatural suspense

Cozy mystery

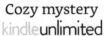

Cold Cases

All my books are available to purchase or borrow from Amazon by clicking the covers or entering Amazon HERE. Thank you so much for your support.
Happy reading until next time

1

Captain Johnson ran through the results one last time.

He took a deep breath as he read the report. He couldn't believe what he was reading. Seventeen soldiers were all facing expulsion for using ephedrine - a controlled substance that was strictly prohibited by the military. Johnson had been in the service for over twenty years, and he had never seen anything like it before. The urine tests had been timed to identify those who had consumed illegal substances during the regiment's summer holidays. The samples for all personnel had been examined for recreational substances such as heroin, cocaine and cannabis. So far so good. But then the 17 soldiers facing expulsion, fell foul of random additional tests for controlled substances such as ephedrine.

He had called a meeting with the seventeen soldiers and their two sergeants. Johnson sat at the head of the table, looking each of them in the eyes.

'I don't need to tell you how serious this is,' he said, his voice stern. 'Using a controlled substance is a breach of trust. It jeopardizes the safety of your fellow soldiers and undermines the integrity of the military. I want to know why you did it.'

The room was silent for a moment, then one of the soldiers spoke up. 'Sir, with all due respect, we didn't know it was a controlled substance. We thought it was protein powder.'

'Need I remind you,' Johnson said, 'that ignorance is no defence. You should have known the ingredients before you put the filthy stuff in your stomachs. Has anyone else got anything to say for themself?'

He was greeted with silence.

'Oh, very well, dismissed,' he barked and stood and turned his back to them as they left.

As Captain Johnson watched the line of soldiers shuffle past the window, he felt a sense of disappointment and frustration gnawing at his gut. He had been in charge of this unit for almost two years now, and he had always prided himself on his ability to keep his men in line. Yet here they were, all 17 of them, caught with their pants down and their urine samples tainted.

He knew he had to act fast, before word spread, and the rest of the unit got wind of what had happened. He quickly huddled with Major Ramirez, and they agreed that swift and decisive action was needed.

'We need to make an example out of them,' Ramirez said, his voice low and serious. 'We can't afford to have drugs in our ranks, not now, not ever.'

Johnson nodded in agreement. He knew what had to be done, but balanced against that was the fact that it would almost certainly ruin the careers of 17 men and severely dent the morale of the regiment. It was not going to be a decision taken lightly.

HAZEL TEN YEARS AGO

Hazel couldn't help but feel his presence everywhere she went.

Every time she turned a corner, she felt like he was waiting for her. Her heart raced and her palms grew sweaty as she walked through the hospital, her eyes darting everywhere, searching for any sign of danger. The corridors were as busy as ever. Patients, doctors, cleaners, porters; they were everywhere. She was never ever really alone. But that fed into what some would call her neurosis. But she called it keeping it real. Her rubber soled shoes squeaked as she walked, tiredness pulling at her limbs, glad another shift was over. Her scrubs were sticking her to sweat, and she was sure she was carrying with her the smells of the ward. She badly needed a shower and the thought of the hot water cascading over her tired limbs, made her quickened her pace.

As she left the brightly lit building behind and began her walk home, she heard footsteps behind her. She quickened her pace, but the footsteps kept up with her. Slowing down, the unknown individual matched her tempo. She stopped and turned around and saw a man in a dark hoodie, his face obscured by shadows.

'Who are you?' she asked, trying, and failing, to keep her voice steady. 'What do you want?'

The man didn't answer, but instead reached into his hoodie and pulled out a knife, glinting in the light from a double decker bus as it rumbled by. She instinctively stepped back, but he advanced on her. She tried to run, but he caught her by the arm and dragged her into the shadows.

She screamed, but no one came. There was no one to come. The man pushed her against the cold concrete wall and pressed the knife to her throat.

'Keep quiet, bitch,' he hissed.

She knew she had to act fast. She mentally searched her pockets for anything that could help her survive the attack. The fingers of her free hand wrapped around something sharp and cold. She pulled out her keys, with the biggest one poking from her fist, between her fingers, and without hesitating plunged it into the man's eye.

He let out a guttural scream of pain and shock and stumbled backward, hands to his damaged face, giving her the opportunity to run. She didn't look back, sprinting as fast as she could until she was sure she was safe.

When she finally reached her apartment, she collapsed onto the floor, her heart racing and body shaking from the adrenaline that had kept her alive.

She couldn't do this. Live in fear for the rest of her life. She wouldn't. She had to take matters into her own hands once and for all. For he was out there, watching her every move, through his circle of sycophants. She'd seen them in the court room, day after day at his trial. The toadies who acted obsequiously towards him, in order to gain advantage. He had a whole gang of them, and any one of them would happily stab, shoot or rape her on his command. And sometimes without his command, if they felt it was what would aid their own journey up the slippery ladder of importance.

But was it really him after her? Or was she being paranoid. Had that just been a random attack? Or something far more sinister? She needed answers.

With shaking hands she pulled out her mobile and pressed the one button she thought she'd never use. When her call was answered, she said, 'It's me... Hazel.'

'Hello, bitch,' growled the voice. 'So, you're still alive then?'

He was behind bars, she knew that, but clearly all that

had achieved was to give her a false sense of security. She'd underestimated him. She wouldn't do it again.

She dropped the phone, and with his laughter ringing from the handset, ran upstairs and grabbed what she had always joked was her, 'go bag'. Just like the spy movies she enjoyed on television.

But this time there was no joke.

It was real.

It was time for her to disappear.

2

Jack arrived on site at Aldershot Garrison just before 7am.

It was a mild morning, already light, with a murder of crows cawing in the trees. The firm he worked for had the contract to dig the footings for a new barracks, the old one having been demolished by a firm from London.

'Ah, there you are, Jack,' came a shout from behind his back and Jack whirled round.

'Oh, it's you, guv,' Jack replied. 'What we up to today?' Jack hitched up his trousers which were trailing in the mud.

'Continuing with the footings, but first I want you to clear up underneath those trees,' and he pointed to a ring of trees around the site, where leaves, rubbish and demolition detritus had collected. 'Scrape the top off it and dump it, would you? The bloody wind's blowing shit everywhere.'

'Sure, guv, on it,' and Jack lumbered off to inspect the area before firing up his digger. He loved his job on days like this, enjoyed working outside when the weather was mild, and birds were singing in the trees. Mind you those bloody crows were doing his head in with their constant cawing. Hopefully they'd bugger off when he fired up the digger. As he waddled further under the canopy of trees and shrubs to investigate the area and make sure there was nothing there that would break his digger, he left the sunshine behind, and gloom enveloped him. He shivered. Shadows played over him. He felt that he was becoming part of the small copse of trees. Panicking he turned and fled for the safety of his yellow machine.

Once in the cab, he took off his hard hat, wiping his floppy brown hair off his face before replacing it. It wouldn't do for him to be found not wearing it. Looking down at himself, he saw his yellow over trousers were splattered with mud, but at least his jacket was clean. Starting the motor, he manipulated the levers, shook himself and got to work, nervously, but diligently, until the first tea break. He wanted to get the job finished as quickly as possible. He still felt unnerved. It was as though the area had a mind of its own and was sending out probing tendrils towards anyone who got too near, and he couldn't wait to finish.

Jack climbed down from his machine, gasping for a cuppa, when something in his bucket caught his eye. It was a dull white colour, sticking out of the soil and the realisation of what it was made him go weak at the knees. Bones. Looking suspiciously like an arm. With a hand at the end of it. Fingers frozen like claws. It was sticking out of the dirt, with the index finger like a directional arrow, pointing at... what? Where the rest of the body was, maybe?

'Ray,' he called to his friend who was passing, 'Go and get the governor would you?'

'Why? What have you found? Buried treasure?' Ray laughed.

'I think I've found a fucking body. Now hurry up!'

After that, things moved remarkably quickly. Being on a military base, the place was soon swarming with soldiers, both in and out of uniform.

Jack was quizzed time and time again by one person after another, until he eventually lost his temper and refused to talk to anyone else.

3

'You're what?' Crane spluttered, as he choked on the mouthful of tea he'd just taken.

'Retiring.'

'Come on, Anderson, you can't be serious!'

'Afraid so, Crane. Look it's the wife, isn't it. And I've done over 25 years.'

'Ages ago,' Crane agreed.

'Exactly and I can't get away with it any longer. I'm out.'

'So… so… what about me?'

'I'm sorry? What did you just say? Are you feeling a bit needy here, Crane? That's not like you!'

'No, no,' Crane blustered. 'Of course not,' he said firmly. But if he was honest, he was feeling needy. Very needy. 'It's just that it won't be the same here without you. Infact, I'd go further by saying-'

'Oh, stop it, Crane, this pained, sulky expression doesn't suit you at all. Grow a pair.'

Crane looked at Anderson in horror, then burst out laughing. 'OK you got me,' he chuckled. 'Sorry, Anderson, but it was just such a shock.'

'I guess so, it came as pretty much a shock to me as well, mate. God knows what I'll do with myself.'

'I expect Mrs Anderson will have that all figured out.'

'That's what worries me. The list of jobs I can do when I retire is growing by the day. Now come on, enough of this, let's grab some lunch.'

Sgt Major Crane (Retired) smiled, but if he was honest with himself, it was a struggle to do so. Anderson had saved him when he'd been retired out of the army due to an accident at work. The damaged leg was a lot better than it was when he was forced to take medical retirement, and he was in a much better place emotionally than he had been when his wife Tina had died. But carrying on in the Aldershot police force as a consultant without Anderson? He couldn't see it somehow. But God knew what the alternative was and for the moment the big man was silent on that one.

All Crane knew was that he was still a relatively young man (okay well into middle age if he was honest) and he had to work. So, a solution would have to be found.

He ran his hand through his dark curls that threatened to take over his head if he didn't keep them short and under control, and scratched at the stubble on his chin, catching his nails on a scar that ran from his cheek to his jaw. Just when things were going well, he'd been bowled yet another curved ball. Looking at Anderson, he could see the fatigue written all over his friend's face. Derek and Jean Anderson had been great friends to Tina and himself over the years and when he'd been made a widower with a young child, Jean had stepped in to help Crane make the correct domestic decisions. He would miss working with Derek everyday but knew that retirement wouldn't alter their friendship. It was Derek's time to lay down his burden and start a new chapter in his life. His Columbo-esq friend deserved the very best of futures and Crane would do all he could to ensure that transition went smoothly.

4

The human remains were in a shallow grave.

As the bones had been found on army land, albeit in a forgotten corner of the Aldershot Garrison, the first port of call was the newly formed Defence Serious Crime Unit (DSCU), an investigative unit launched to handle serious criminal offences. A tri-service initiative to which WO2 Billy Williams of the previously known Special Investigations Branch had been incorporated into. Billy was the senior advisor to the officer commanding Major Rhodes, and also in command of the Aldershot sub-unit. A strapping young man in his late 30's, Billy was now several grades higher in rank than when he had first arrived at Aldershot and worked under Sgt Major Crane.

Billy ran his hand through his hair, pushing his shock of blond locks away from his forehead and buttoned up his suit jacket against the blustery wind that buffeted him as his got out of his car. He'd driven over from Provost Barracks where he was based. Military Investigators didn't wear uniform and Billy still favoured the dark suit and white shirt look that Sgt Major Crane had instilled in him. Billy looked around at the strange area. He'd thought he knew every inch of Aldershot Garrison, but it appeared not, as he arrived at the out of the way plot of land where the contractors were working.

Although DSCU had their own forensic expertise, Billy had felt that a civilian forensic anthropologist would be a better call for this case. If they really were human bones, then the soil around them would have to be very carefully examined and brushed off each one. Jogging up to the man who looked like he was in charge, due to his clip board and very worried expression, Billy identified himself. He was taken over to the digger involved and introduced to the driver, Jack. Looking into the bucket of the digger at the hand and arm poking out of the soil in it, he had to agree with Jack the digger driver who'd said that the whole thing was as creepy as fuck. Again, he refrained from touching the bones, or freeing them from the bucket. He shivered and turned away, his mind full of questions.

Who had they just found? A civilian or a squaddy?

Come to that, male or female?

Would they find one body or two?

And when had the victim died?

He knew it would be several days before he got any answers, if at all. And it would also be several days before work could recommence on this section of the garrison. Something he was just about to share with the site foreman.

He knew it wouldn't go down well.

5

As was protocol, Billy telephoned the CID department of the civilian police.

He got Detective Inspector Anderson on the line and after Billy had shared his news about the body in the shrubs, Anderson told Billy some news of his own.

'Retiring?' spluttered Billy. 'You? What will you do all day?'

'That's what Crane said but I think Mrs Anderson has that covered.'

Billy couldn't tell if Anderson was pleased or not, as he seemed as stoic as ever. But his overriding thought was, what would happen to Crane?

He couldn't resist the question and out loud he said, 'What will happen to Crane?'

'I'm not sure yet,' said Anderson. 'We've offered for him to stay here under the new DI, Lawrence Wood, but at the moment he's not made up his mind.'

That got Billy thinking. Was there any way he could utilise his old boss' skills? Would the powers that be allow it? Possibly... maybe...

Standing he looked through his office window to the new set-up that was taking shape in Provost Barracks. It was to be a larger unit than before, as befitted the tri-service badge, with its own forensic team on site. Previously Army investigators had been trained in forensic collection and had their own kit. However, with the advances in the science it was felt that specialists would be a better fit. A laboratory was being kitted out and a new computer hub for the intelligence boffin who would be arriving in a day or two.

After mulling his idea over, and looking at it from all angles, he went to see Major Rhodes. Once he'd brought his officer commanding up to speed on the body under the trees, he mentioned that DI Anderson was retiring.

'He'll be a loss, I image. What's happening to his staff?' asked Rhodes.

'They can stay, but there's no news on Crane making a decision.' Billy dropped Crane's name into the conversation, trying for innocence, but not sure he'd nailed it.

'Crane?' Rhodes head snapped up. 'Do you mean Sgt Major Crane? The one that was medically retired?'

'One and the same, boss,' agreed Billy. He drew a deep breath and decided to plunge in. 'He's been working with the Aldershot police for some time now, as a consultant. And as he might be free, I was wondering if we could make use of his considerable experience. Have him working on army cold cases, for example. God knows we could do with some help here.'

Rhodes appeared to mull that over. He got up from his desk and wandered over to the window. Turning back, he faced Billy and said, 'What are you up to? What's your current case load?'

'The woman under the bushes is one. Crane could do that as it will be a cold case. I'm mired down with this drugs scandal. There's also a couple of thefts on the garrison, oh and a couple of alleged assault and battery.'

'How many cold cases?'

'You don't want to know.'

'Billy....'

'Over 50.'

'What?' Rhodes looked horrified and sat back down behind his desk with a thump.

'Looks like the incumbents of the office over the past few years either haven't tackled older cases or not brought all of their new ones to a satisfactory conclusion.'

'Shit.'

'My thoughts exactly, boss. It doesn't bear thinking about should the press get hold of this while they're reporting on our latest body... After all we want them to think the best of our new tri-service arrangements. We wouldn't want to start off on the wrong foot.'

Billy had to endure Rhodes' close scrutiny as the officer debated internally. 'And if we give him a go? What would the press say to that?'

As Billy tried to speak, Rhodes held up his hand. 'That was a rhetorical question, Billy.'

Finally, he made a note in his daybook and said, 'Alright, I'll push it up the chain of command. Should have a decision for you by tomorrow afternoon.'

'Thanks, boss,' said Billy flashing a grin and leaving before Rhodes changed his mind.

Infact the decision came through much earlier than Billy could have imagined. As he was just leaving the office at the end of the day, he was stopped by the ringing of the telephone on his desk. Sighing and dropping his bag on the floor, he walked around his desk to answer the phone.

'Ah, Williams,' said Rodes. 'Glad I've caught you. I've agreement on Crane. But...'

Billy thought he knew what was coming next.

'He is your responsibility. Do you understand?' Rhodes said sternly. 'Don't forget he's a maverick and if he fucks up, then you have fucked up. Conversely, if the arrangement works well, then you will be considered to have made the right decision and it will go on your report. OK?'

'Understood, sir, and thank you.'

'Don't thank me. I'm not altogether happy with the situation but Crane still has a good reputation here. There is a feeling that a brilliant career was cut short when he had that awful accident and that the army owe him, so we must do whatever we can. Blocking this move would seem petty. Anyway, it's now up to you.'

Before Billy could reply, Rhodes had put the phone down.

'You've done what?' Emma spluttered when he told her his news over dinner.

'Got permission for Crane to join the new unit.'

'Are you mad?'

'No, Emma, I'm not. I can't think of anyone else I'd rather work with.'

'Well, you two do have a long history together,' she said, picking up the crying baby and handing it to Billy. 'Hold her while I get a bottle.'

Billy began jogging the baby on his knee. 'You'll soon get to meet your Uncle Crane,' he cooed. 'What a treat that will be. And Daniel of course.'

The now silent baby looked up at her father's face.

'That's right,' Billy said. 'Uncle Crane and Daniel. What fun you'll have!'

Emma returned as he was chatting nonsense to his daughter. 'Here,' she said, with a smile on her face. 'You can feed her while I finish my dinner.'

Billy grabbed the bottle and changed the baby to his other arm. She opened and closed her mouth like a little bird waiting to be fed. As soon as he put the teat to her lips, she began to suck.

'You have this knack of calming her down,' Emma said. 'I can't seem to manage it like you do.'

'Ah, but I'm not here all the time, am I? So, I'm more of a novelty.'

'Ah, and I'm the skivvy who does her bidding.'

Billy laughed. 'If the shoe fits…' then ducked as Emma threw a soft toy at his head.

As he kissed his daughter's head, Billy wondered, had he made a brilliant, bold move wanting Crane to join the unit?

Or one that would prove to be his downfall?

6

Sat in the garden of his Victorian house in Ash, Crane sipped on a bottle of beer.

Daniel was in bed. The au pair on a night out. He was free to try and put his thoughts in order. On Crane's mind all the time was his future. Or lack of it. Let's face it he was on the rubbish heap. Washed out. Thrown away.

He ran his fingers through his dark hair, that now had a good sprinkling of grey. Picking up his beer he had to acknowledge that it wasn't really Anderson's fault for retiring and bringing this situation about. Nor was it the fault of the new DI who didn't really want Crane anywhere near his current cases. He had his own team that he was bringing with him to Aldershot and Crane doubted he'd fit in.

It rather looked as though he should stop worrying about people who didn't want him and focus on those who did. It was just that he hadn't come across any of them yet.

The doorbell interrupted his thoughts, and he climbed out of his chair and went to answer it. Annoyed at being stopped dead in his musings he grumbled, 'OK, I'm coming.'

He flung open the door to find not someone canvassing the area for double glazing, or burglar alarms, or God forbid the local elections, but the welcome sight of Billy Williams, dressed in civvies. He was obviously still in the army if his short sharp haircut was anything to go by. He looked muscular in his polo shirt and jeans with the body of someone that took his gym work seriously.

'Billy Williams,' Crane said. 'As I live and breathe. What the hell brings you down here?'

'I'm back in Aldershot,' Billy said. 'So, I thought I'd look you up.'

'Well come in, come in,' and Crane opened the door wider to allow Billy in. 'Go through to the garden and I'll bring you a beer. I take it you're off duty as you're in civvies.'

'A beer would be great, thanks.'

Crane followed Billy into the garden, who grabbed a seat and put it opposite Crane as they sat at the small iron table and chairs.

'Welcome back,' Crane said. 'What's happening on the garrison these days? I've not worked a crime with the SIB for some time now.'

Crane had been the Sgt Major in charge of the special investigation branch of the military police on Aldershot Garrison. At that time Billy had been a Sergeant on Crane's team.

Billy explained to Crane about the new Defence Services Unit and that he'd been moved back to Aldershot to take over the sub-unit.

'What rank are you now, then?

Billy looked embarrassed. 'I've just been promoted.'

'Yes? To?'

'WO2.'

'Bloody hell, well done, lad, well done. Of course, it's all because you worked with me and I taught you everything you know,' Crane laughed.

'Talking of that…'

Crane quietened and looked bemused. The mood seemed to have turned from frivolity to seriousness in a single breath.

Billy hesitated, then said, 'How do you fancy working with me again?'

'Working with you?' Crane exclaimed. 'How on earth would that be possible? Have you forgotten I'm out of the army? Thrown on the rubbish heap in my prime.'

'Come on, Crane, just hear me out, yes?' At a nod from Crane he continued, 'It's just that I've walked into a backlog of cold cases and I really, really need some help.'

'Yes, but…'

Billy put up his hand to stop Crane voicing his thoughts, making him listen. 'I've had permission to take you on, on a consultancy basis.'

Crane was stunned. There was a pregnant pause and then he said, 'Rather like the police?'

'Exactly like the police. What do you think?'

'Well to be honest,' said Crane, 'I'm not sure what to think.'

'You've got to do something, I expect. The house and your boy and his nanny all have to be paid for.'

'Tina's life insurance payment paid the mortgage off on the house and I've still got a lot of the payment from being invalided out of the army,' Crane said.

'And how long would that last without working?'

'Okay, okay, so you have a point. But moving on, why would I do it? To be honest I'm not sure about going back to the constraints of the army. God only knows the trouble I had with them when I was in the SIB.'

'But you won't be.'

'Won't be what?'

'Constrained. You're a consultant who is somewhat a maverick.'

A big grin split Crane's face at that one.

'Rhodes' use of the word maverick, not mine,' smiled Billy.

'Look, are you sure about this?' asked Crane. 'Really sure?'

'Crane, you're the best investigator I know. You'll be reporting to me and dealing with cold cases only. You'll have access to all our facilities and personnel. Come on, Crane. The families involved in these cases need closure. They want justice. And you're bloody good at justice. Look what you did to get justice for Tina.'

Unable to speak for a moment, at the use of Tina's name, Crane took a large gulp of his beer. He thought it would be a wonderful thing, to try and get justice for those families and soldiers who had not had any. That was a big factor for Crane - justice. He remembered how he'd felt when Tina had died, and he'd begun investigating her death. He'd wanted justice for her. He'd wanted to see her killer behind bars. He'd caught the low life and justice had been served. The victims in the cold cases deserved that too.

Plus, Crane was acutely aware that Billy had gone out on a limb to help him, so maybe he could help Billy in return? Repay the debt? He looked at Billy who was looking at him with hope in his eyes. How could Crane turn down a friend? And a friend in need at that.

7

Crane wasn't a policeman in the Aldershot Police.

That stark fact meant that he didn't have to give any sort of notice and after a conversation with Anderson, was able to report to Billy's office the following Monday.

Dressed in his usual SIB attire of dark suit, white shirt and dark tie (rather like Men in Black according to his son), he collected a temporary pass from the soldier on sentry duty at the barracks, parked his car and walked across the car park with some trepidation. Everything looked the same but was very different. Since he'd left the army with a damaged back and leg, his son had grown and was now in school. His wife was dead. He was on au pair number 3. But what was still the same was that Crane was an investigator. Full stop. He stood up for the victims of crime. Worked as hard as he could to give them closure. It didn't matter to him if the victim was army or civilian. He gave 110% to the case. But that's what got him into trouble most of the time. Billy was right when he described Crane as a maverick. A person who showed independence of thought and action, especially by refusing to adhere to the policies of a group to which he or she belonged. But he was also dogged in his pursuit of justice.

He doubted the army had changed fundamentally. There might be a new tri-service department made up of Army, Navy and Air Force investigators, which should work well for pooling information, but would it really? Army was army, navy was navy (and called themselves the senior service) and the air force always had that air of superiority. But as far as Crane was concerned, the British Army was the best of the three.

He hoped the other staff at Provost Barracks in Aldershot

wouldn't see him as too much of an outsider. He clearly wasn't after their jobs, being too old and too disabled. He would like to be viewed as an asset that was taking some of the strain of cases from them. Crane almost crossed his fingers as he entered the barracks.

Billy was enthusiastically effusive upon Crane's arrival. Maybe he was nervous, Crane thought. Wondering if he'd done the right thing? Hoping to God he hadn't made the biggest mistake of his career? But as for Crane himself, he was nervous but would never show it. Shoulders back, smile on his face, immaculate clothes, stand tall. Proud of who he was and his achievements, but not ram them down other's throats.

He met various members of the team. A couple of forensic guys pouring over their equipment in the newly built laboratory barely looked up when Crane and Billy went past. The office manager was no longer Kim, but a newly promoted, fresh faced young man by the name of Lewis. Two investigators were in a hushed conversion but broke off to be introduced. Two Lance Corporals; a woman called Nowak and a man who went by the name of Cash.

Towards the end of the open plan layout was Billy's office, Crane's desk and a final person hiding behind what looked like a bank of computer screens.

'Dudley,' called Billy, 'Say hello to our latest recruit.'

A face peered round a screen. 'For God's sake, Billy, can't you leave me alone for five minutes?'

Recognising the name and the face and the voice, Crane spluttered, 'No, I don't believe it!'

The face of Dudley-Jones popped up exclaiming something similar. 'What the bloody hell are you doing here, Crane?'

'I could say the same to you,' said Crane shaking Dudley-Jones' hand.

He remembered the last conversation he'd had with Billy about Dudley-Jones when his wife, Tina had died, and they'd needed a technical analyst.

'I recommend Dudley-Jones.' Billy had said.

'What? The computer analyst who helped when the athletes

were on the Garrison and when you were on that bloody train?'

'The very same. He's seconded to the Special Investigations Branch for a while.'

'So, he's here? On the Garrison?'

'Yeah.'

'Well, I never,' said Crane. 'I always liked him. He's a bit scrawny for a soldier, mind.'

'But bloody good at his job.'

'Yes, he is. And you think he'll want to help?'

'I can guarantee it.'

'Really?'

'Boss, he'd do anything for you, thinks you walk on water.'

Crane snapped back to the present and asked Jones, 'How come you're still here?'

'Not still here but brought back by Billy who conned me into it,' he grinned. 'More to the point why are you here?'

Billy stepped in. 'Crane here is our newest recruit, our cold case specialist.'

Dudley's eyes widened. 'Really?'

'Really,' said Crane. 'We must catch up over a beer or two, but for now I best get on. Don't want to upset the boss,' he added with a wink.

He followed Billy into his office, leaving the door open. Sitting behind his desk, Billy said, 'You can use Dudley for any research, but I don't want you monopolising him. Is that clear?'

'Crystal,' replied Crane, although he unobtrusively had his fingers crossed. Who knew what info Crane would need going forward? And probably Dudley would be the only one who could provide it.

Billy slid a folder across the top of his desk to Crane.

'Your first cold case. Enjoy.'

8

The morning sun shone across Aldershot as an unnerving news report began to break.

Word of a body found had travelled quickly and questions were being asked across the town. Diane Chambers, now Editor of the Aldershot News, was determined to uncover the truth, as fear and confusion spread among her fellow citizens. She wanted answers, so she needed to go to where the action was.

That turned out to be a building site on the edge of Aldershot Garrison. A nowhere place that that been left to the elements over the years and was now being regenerated with modern executive homes that wouldn't help the people of the town. Only incomers who had the money to pay the exorbitant price wanted by developers selling the utopian dream.

Except that Aldershot had a drug and homeless problem, as well as hundreds of Ghurkhas and their families trying to eke out a modest pension, far from home and everything they held dear.

Diane Chambers smelled of stale cigarettes and cold coffee, an odour so familiar that she could barely smell it on herself anymore. At times such as this, she felt like a ghost. Shimmering like heat caught on water's surface, her body reflecting the world around her as she passed through it without it touching her. Her skin cool and waxy, her nails red and newly polished. Diane felt her journalist's credentials in her jacket pocket. The notebook she favoured; the paper smooth, and worn, the plastic laminate cover hard.

As Diane hurried to the building site, all she knew was that a John Doe with no identification had been discovered. That was the bland truth of it. Yet she knew there would be a human story behind the harsh words, and it was her job to find it and tell the tale.

Diane looked around at the building site, which she imagined had fallen silent as the news of the body being found had spread. She stood still among the scaffolding, which cast rectangular shadows over the construction workers. A mound of dirt and cement sacks leaned to one side of a partially built wall like a small mountain. The air was hot, full of dust and grumbling voices and stray bits of gravel that crunched underfoot. She looked up at the sky. The clouds had blown in and the air was pregnant with rain.

She took in a sharp breath and let it out slowly. A crew of men stood around, talking quietly amongst themselves. Their silhouettes were like broken sentences on a page, bits of meaning that would never be read.

She fancied she could see Sgt Major Crane, standing apart from everyone, his back to her, as he had done so many times in the past. Staring down into his coffee cup, lost in thought. In another time and place, she might have been able to touch him, just by reaching out her hand. She shook her head to dispel the image. What was she thinking? Crane was no longer with the Hampshire police. Anderson was out and therefore so was Crane.

Never again would they lock horns. Her wanting the story and him determined not to give an inch.

But that wasn't her problem. It was her job to report on the finding of human bones in a shallow grave on Aldershot Garrison and that was exactly what she was going to do.

9

Crane left Billy's office.

He grabbed a coffee from the small kitchen and sat at his empty desk. The rate of decomposition of a body was largely dependent upon the cause of death, the weight of the deceased and other environmental factors. Bodies decayed at a faster rate if they had been exposed to the elements or wildlife, or if they were in warm environments, or if they were under water.

Crane knew that forensic scientists had created body farms to study human decomposition rates under various conditions. Major Martin had further stated in his report that their skeleton could have been killed anywhere between 1 year and several years ago.

They had decided that their skeleton was female. Her age at death was estimated to be 30. She took frequent exercise, smoked and was lacking in dental hygiene. Cause of death was expected to be from strangulation. They had managed to extract DNA from the bones and as a result they now had a positive identification.

Before he did anything else, Crane wanted to visit the site where their victim was found in her shallow grave. It was only a few minutes' drive from Provost Barracks, but still, not somewhere Crane was familiar with. Following the instructions in the file, Crane arrived at the building site. Parking his car on the side of the road, he wandered over to the spot where the body had been buried.

He had to agree with the digger driver's description of the scene. Tall trees swished in the wind, but with an air of menace that was hard to ignore. The shade was dense, almost black and the shadow palpable. There was a sense of evil pervading the area, which made Crane shiver involuntarily. Her killer had to be found, Crane was in no doubt of that. And the killer of the poor child that was in her. Unborn. Clinging onto its mother for its very lifeblood. And when that dried up and the mother died, so did the baby.

A search done by Dudley-Jones had come up with someone from the Garrison reported missing by her husband some years ago. Crane recalled his discussion with Billy earlier.

'So, he was army then?' Crane had asked Billy.

'No, she was. That makes it our problem.'

'And the DNA check?' asked Crane.

'She'd voluntarily provided a DNA reference sample, as did most soldiers. These are used solely for the identification of deceased Service personnel and to reduce delays for grieving families, when other methods of identification such as visual and dental are not available. Such DNA reference samples are taken by consent, which means the consent given before death remains valid for a DNA sample intended for use after death.'

Realising there was nothing else to be obtained from the burial site, and failing to notice Diane Chambers watching him, Crane returned to the barracks.

HAZEL EIGHT YEARS AGO

Changing her identity had worked like a charm.

After she'd found out who was trying to kill her, it was a no brainer. Having obtained a new identity, Hazel joined up, for, as she was surfing the internet one day, up popped an advert for the army. They'd wanted nurses who would retrain as emergency medical staff. Not what she'd meant to do with her life at the time, but later realised it was the best move she'd ever made.

She'd signed on the dotted line and within weeks she was doing basic training and issued with a uniform. With her hair cut short and coloured a shiny conker colour she'd looked very different from her previous look of long hair, coloured blond.

After the attack, she'd wished she'd had the guts and the strength to turn him in, but she knew her limitations and hadn't want to push her luck. Also, she was afraid of him. A drug dealer, with many contacts and money to burn, she knew he'd find her if she stayed in civvy street. As it was, with her name change, appearance change and location change, she figured she was far enough removed from her past as she could get.

So, leaving her worries behind, she'd immersed herself in the army. Her training as a nurse had been done in her maiden name and had been brought up to date by a very helpful lady in the office of the university, who'd seemed to understand that Hazel was running from an abusive husband and had a desperate need to get away. Therefore, she'd gladly supplied a new certificate with just the surname change.

It looked as though there was brightness on the horizon at last.

10

Upon Crane's returned to the barracks he requested access to anything collected from the burial site, from the forensic specialists.

'Here you are,' said Bob Hunt, who had introduced himself as the lead forensic technician.

Crane took himself off to a quiet space on the work bench and opened the lid of the clear plastic box he'd been handed. He had half expected bones and was relived not to have any in the box. That meant that her remains would be returned to the family for burial.

But what had been found, and was in the box, was the remains of a handbag.

Crane gently picked it out of the box with gloved hands. There were still bits of soil covering the fabric of the bag. It appeared to be leather, which was probably the reason it had survived for so long under the earth.

Crane opened the zip, having to tug in places where the fastener was rusted. Then peered inside. To find… nothing.

Huffing in frustration he began to feel all the sides of the bag from the inside. Maybe something of use had been left inside by mistake. It seemed to Crane that the contents had been emptied by her killer, to help cover his or her tracks. As his fingers traced the lining of the bag, he came across a rectangular shape. Grabbing a torch, he turned it on and carefully examined all the sides once more. The rectangular shape was caught between the lining and the leather. With a scalpel Crane carefully cut the lining to free the shape which he slowly teased out of its hiding place.

Placing the rectangle of plastic into a forensic bag of its own, he closed the handbag and returned it to the box. Looking at the faded and yellowed piece of plastic, Crane realised he had just found a driving licence.

This time he grabbed a magnifying glass. Peering through it, he found a photograph of a youngster by the name of Hazel Young. Not Hazel Cooper, their victim. But the photograph looked like a younger version of her. Which was correct? The date on it was when their victim was approximately 18. And the address? North Street, Wallsend. Was this an army address? Crane very much doubted it. It was more likely that he'd found that their deceased soldier had been leading a double life.

He went to speak to Dudley-Jones, who saw him coming.

'Yes, Crane, what do you want? I guess it's not to check on my mental health or my social life.'

Crane grinned. 'Am I that obvious?'

'More than that obvious. So, what do you want?'

Crane showed him the driving licence.

'Who's that?' the analyst asked.

'Our dead girl. Turns out she had a life before the army.'

'Along with another name.'

'Right. Assuming that was her maiden name...'

'You want me to check out her name and address on this licence?' Dudley-Jones finished for Crane.

'Yes. Um, is that alright? Is this what you'll do for me?'

'Are you feeling alright, Crane?'

'Eh?'

'I've never known you ask before. Normally you just bark out orders.'

'Ah, well, I've mellowed a bit these days.'

'That is positively horizontal for you. Come back, Crane, all is forgiven.'

Crane grinned. 'Well now you've put me in my place, get on with it, would you? I haven't got all bloody day!'

Crane ran away as Dudley-Jones pelted him with balled up paper.

In a storage cupboard Crane found a white board on a frame

with wheels. He decided to commandeer it and wheeled it to his desk, placing it against the wall of Billy's office – the one without a window. Going back to the cupboard he grabbed a set of marker pens.

By the time he'd taken the cap off the black pen, Dudley-Jones called out, 'So, our victim is called Hazel Cooper, the woman who died and was found buried on the Aldershot Garrison. Dave Cooper was her husband. She put her maiden name as Hazel Winter, but I have found evidence that her maiden name was actually Hazel Young as per your driving licence. Dave Cooper's current address is unknown, but he is believed to still be in Aldershot. The police would love to talk to him about drug smuggling. Hazel Young's mother is Cora Young, and she still lives at that address in Wallsend.'

'So, what is the name Hazel Winter all about?'

'Sorry, Crane, not found anything on that yet. I'm waiting for Newcastle to get back to me.'

'OK thanks for that. I'd better go to Newcastle and break the news to her mother that her daughter is dead.'

'Why not ask someone nearer to call in?'

'Because, Dudley-Jones, you learn a lot about a person when you tell them that their child, or husband, or wife, has unfortunately died.'

'Oh, and you think this Cora Young might give you more information if you meet face to face. You old charmer, you.'

'Well, if you've got it, flaunt it,' said Crane and sauntered off to the coffee machine.

11

Crane knew how far away Newcastle was.

He was a Geordie, but one that hadn't been back home for many years. As a result, nothing had prepared him for the actual journey. In the end he'd decided to fly to Newcastle because of the threat of rail strikes. It was a Saturday and he wanted to give himself a good chance of finding Cora Young at home.

The flight from London Heathrow took about an hour and a half, and finally the taxi he'd taken from Newcastle Airport, pulled up outside the address in Wallsend.

His knock at the door of a small Victorian terraced house, was answered by a woman with dark hair scraped back from her face, red lipstick on and a cigarette hanging from her lips.

'I don't want anything,' she shrieked. 'Nothing! Don't you lot understand!'

'Mrs Young?' asked Crane. 'Can I speak to you about your daughter?'

Cora Young eyed Crane suspiciously. 'You're not selling anything?'

'No.'

'You're not trying to sell me double glazing?'

No, ma'am.'

'You're not collecting for charity?'

'No.'

'Who the hell are you then?' she sucked on the cigarette, her cheeks disappearing as the end of the cigarette glowed.

'Tom Crane, ma'am.'

'Polis?'

'Army. Do you have a daughter, Hazel?'

'Yes, yes I do,' she said, looking bemused.

'In that case, may I come in?'

'Army? What the hell has the army got to do with my Hazel?'

'If I could come in, I'll explain everything. Mrs Young people are starting to look.'

Cora Young poked her head around her door like a turtle from a shell and looked up and down the street, finding that what Crane had said was true.

'Bloody gossips, the lot of them,' she grumbled and turned and walked into the bowels of the house.

As she'd left the door open, Crane figured he should follow her and did so.

'Sit down,' she barked as they walked into the living room. It reeked of cigarettes and Crane spied a full ashtray on the mantle over the fire.

They each took an armchair, as the sofa was full of newspapers, magazines and unopened letters.

'Is there anyone else in the house,' Crane asked. 'Mr Young, perhaps?'

'No, he died some years back. Hazel left home when she was 18 and her brother Roman two years afterwards. No heard much from either of them since. But you said you were from the Army. What? Is she AWOL or whatever the hell you call it?'

'I'm afraid not, Mrs Young. We have reason to believe that Hazel is dead.'

Mrs Young was stunned into silence. Crane let her be until she felt able to speak again.

Visibly swallowing her emotion, she said, 'I always wondered what had happened to her, but dead wasn't what I had in mind. More married with kids, you know. Have you found her then?'

Tears shone in her eyes, then broke free and rolled down her cheeks unchecked. She seemed to have aged 10 years in the last 10 minutes. Her eyes were hollow and lifeless, her skin a strange hue of grey. He noticed that the backs of her hands were shaking slightly making the liver spots appear to wobble.

'Yes, I'm sorry to have to tell you that her body was found

while we were demolishing a barracks in Aldershot.'

'Aldershot? Barracks? Wait did you said demolishing them?'

Deflecting the questions, Crane said, 'Mrs Young, when did you last see your daughter?'

'Oh, let's see, she was 21, I think. Wasn't living here, of course.'

'She wasn't?'

'No, she was married to a bloke, Winter his name was. Never liked him myself, but still he gave me a grandchild.'

'A grandchild?'

'Why yes, didn't you know?'

Crane shook his head. Then said, 'So, you have a living grandchild that your daughter left behind when she disappeared?'

Cora paused and then said, 'What do you mean, living? What are you talking about? What have you found?'

'Hazel was found dead in a shallow grave. She was pregnant when she was killed.'

'Hang on, are you with the police?' she asked again, looking at Crane with renewed suspicion.

'Not exactly, ma'am,' Crane said. 'I'm an investigator for the army, see,' he held out his ID. 'My name is Sgt Major Crane.'

'So Hazel was in….'

'The army, yes ma'am. For five years before she died. She was called Hazel Cooper.'

'And do you know who killed her?'

'No, I'm sorry, I don't, but that's what I intend to find out.'

'Wait a minute,' Cora said. 'How do you know it's her? If she was found in a grave, like?'

'Her DNA.'

'Oh, I've heard about that, seen it on the telly, like. So, there's no doubt then. It really is her?' Her voice was a whisper, yet thick with emotion, all hope gone, drained away.

'Yes, it's her and no there's no doubt about it. Her DNA was on file, as are most soldier's. '

'So why did you think she was my daughter? What with a different name and everything?

'Buried with her was a driving licence. I found it caught in the lining of her handbag. So, I did some digging and...'

'Arrived at my door.'

Crane nodded.

'I didn't have a clue why, or where she'd gone,' said Cora, her voice heavy with regret.

'Were there any arguments that might have triggered her leaving?'

'We all thought she'd been suffering from post-natal depression. Her daughter was only 10 months old when Hazel disappeared. That's not natural, is it? A mother doesn't leave a young baby surely?'

'What happened to the baby?'

'We brought her up, me and her granddad.'

'So, to clarify, you had no idea where she'd gone nor that she'd changed her name.'

'No, I just said didn't I.'

But Crane wasn't sure he believed her. There was a hardness there. In her eyes. Who or what had Hazel been running from? For Crane believed that this was what it was all about. She ran away. Not to join the French foreign legion, but the British Army. She clearly wanted to be swallowed up by something or someone bigger than herself and anyway who would have thought that's what she'd do?

'Young was her maiden name?'

Cora nodded.

'That's what I figured,' Crane agreed. 'What about her husband?'

'Winter? He's gone 'un all. Currently residing at His Majesty's Pleasure.'

That's when Crane realised the defiance in Cora Young's face was a message – don't judge me or my daughter. We did the best we could under the circumstances.

'Winter was a bully?' Crane asked.

'That's putting it mildly,' she answered. 'Evil, that's what he was. An evil, controlling, bastard.'

12

Crane flew home.

He was lucky enough not to have anyone sitting next to him. He had the window seat and then a spare seat, with a woman at the aisle end. She was of indeterminable age with a trim figure and short hair. She looked vaguely familiar. It was only when he got his file out that he realised she looked like his victim. Looking more closely he realised the woman was older than he'd first imagined with wrinkles by her eyes and around her mouth. It was merely his mind playing tricks on him. In the cold light of his realisation, she didn't look like Hazel Cooper at all.

Shaking his head at his mistake, he knuckled down to work, got out his pad and made notes on his visit to Newcastle. Somehow that visit had raised more questions than answers. Had Hazel run away from an abusive husband? Did he find her? Or was he a red herring? Crane realised he needed more information and when he got back to the office on Monday, he'd have several tasks to do.

First of all, he needed Hazel's service record. Where had she been? What did she put on her army application? Where was her passport? Had she married David Cooper whilst she was in the army? Was she still married when she died? Where did she live? How many months pregnant was she?

He needed to check the post-mortem. Why was she and the baby killed? He knew unplanned killing, done in anger. But why? And where was it done? There in the shrubbery where she was buried? Or at home? On the Garrison while she was on duty?

What had happened when she couldn't be found? From the file it appeared that nothing more was done. That didn't compute to Crane. But then they must have thought there was nothing to be done. The officers just thought she'd gone AWOL.

The army quarter her and her husband lived in was now let out to another family. In due course Crane would have to interview her husband. If only he could be found that was. He seemed to have gone AWOL himself.

All the thoughts were giving Crane a headache and he massaged his temples which did absolutely nothing. He'd missed a Saturday with Daniel which didn't make him feel good. He was determined to do something nice with the child tomorrow. He'd leave his worries about the case until Monday. So, he settled back and closed his eyes. He was asleep in minutes.

13

Over the last year an increasing number of soldiers have tested positive for banned substances during compulsory drug testing.

However, many have claimed, that the only substances they have ever taken are sports supplements, which were taken to improve their fitness and strength – two vital characteristics in a soldier.

Billy threw the Aldershot News back onto his desk. Yes, yes, he knew all about it. But how had the Aldershot News found out about it? Where had they got their information from?

He knew that the Ministry of Defence had made instructional videos for new recruits joining up, stressing that supplements encouraged by gym owners, were just a short cut and not really necessary. They could even be a waste of money. Plus, there was often no guarantee that a manufacturer had not added a banned substance and failed to provide the details on the label. Everyone should know that the Armed Forces official policy on supplements was simply that they were not needed – soldiers just need to eat plenty of nutritious food. If, however, someone chose to take a supplement, they should first verify that it was safe. For all forms of anabolic steroids were illegal and should never be taken.

Billy felt a stress headache forming. Drugs. What had turned a routine urine test into a nightmare, was ephedrine. There were 17 soldiers so far who had tested positive for performance enhancing chemicals. It was a nightmare. Especially as they were all pleading ignorance, including their Sgt Major who had also tested positive. They claimed they'd unwittingly taken ephedrine contained in supplements.

It came down to the age-old adage. Ignorance is not a defence. It was on the soldiers to check that whatever they were taking did not include any banned anabolic steroids. Billy loved gym work as much as the next man, but he'd never taken a supplement. Not once. For huge muscles were not a sign of strength insomuch as a they were a hindrance. It was no good having thighs like tree trunks if you were bursting out of your uniform and finding that running around, carrying equipment, ended up causing chaffed legs.

But despite all that, it was up to him to prepare a report for the officers of the men currently on charge. What was to be done with them? Was it worth bouncing them out of the army? Was it worth wasting the thousands of pounds per man that it had cost to train them? Or should the army have a clear policy – out means out, as some regiments have done. Or maybe a more lenient punishment, say losing a rank would work better. At the moment it seemed that nothing was clear, not even the bloody punishment. Grabbing his coat, Billy decided he needed fresh air.

Maybe Pardre Symmonds would be taking a turn around the rugby field and he just might be able to help Billy with some clear thinking. Plus the fact that the Pardre and his wife Kim, would be interested to hear of his new recruit. The thought brought a smile to his face and a jaunt in his step as he left the office.

14

Monday morning came round soon enough.

Crane decided to visit the house where Hazel Cooper had lived with her husband. He needed to talk to her neighbours, who would also be mothers and whose husbands would be of the same rank as each other. As the men progressed up the ladder, they would be entitled to bigger and better housing. Along with a higher salary, of course. Hazel Cooper and her husband had lived in a general quarter, as befitted her rank of corporal.

Crane found a clutch of mothers, all pushing prams with infants of indeterminable age within them, having just dropped older children off at school. In response to his question of who had lived next door to the Coopers, there was only one mother who knew what he was talking about. She identified herself as Jill Doors, wife of a Lance Corporal. Crane walked with Jill back to her house.

'I remember Hazel,' said Jill, who was dressed in navy leggings and a t-shirt with a puffa-jacket on over the top in a vivid pink. 'Hard to forget really.'

Crane thought Jill's jacket would be hard to forget. Mentally admonishing himself to keep his mind on the conversation, he said, 'Why is that?'

'Because they had a baby under the age of one, I'd say. And it was always bloody crying. She would shout and scream at it. To be honest I was going to ring child services or welfare, it was getting that bad.'

That thought troubled Crane more than he liked to admit. He mustn't get emotional, he chided himself silently. He must maintain a calm, in control exterior, despite whatever emotional disturbance was raging within. And so, he continued with his questions.

'And David Cooper, what was he like?'

'Didn't see much of him, not that I saw at any rate. They kept themselves to themselves, the Coopers, mind.'

'Why wasn't Hazel back at work?'

'Her maternity leave wasn't up yet.'

Crane recalled that he'd checked up on the current maternity leave rules and found that up to 52 weeks of maternity leave was possible. It was made up of 26 weeks ordinary maternity leave (OML) plus 26 weeks additional maternity leave (AML). During the 26 weeks OML Hazel was entitled to full normal pay and the first 13 weeks of AML were paid at the standard rate of statutory maternity pay (SMP). The remaining 13 weeks were unpaid. He conceded that the longer Hazel had gone without working, the more family finances were shrinking. And that was often a pressure cooker moment for a lot of couples.

'And then she just upped and disappeared,' Jill Doors said.

'With David and the child?'

'No, on her own. One day she was there and the next she wasn't. David said that as far as he knew she'd left him holding the baby, literally.'

'You mean she didn't take the kid?'

'No. Strangest thing I ever saw. Lovely little boy he was as well. As least when he was away from her and her bloody shouting.'

'Did you know that she was pregnant when she disappeared?'

'No, she hadn't said anything to me. Mind you we weren't close, so she wouldn't have.'

'Do you know where David Cooper is now?' asked Crane, mindful of the fact that they hadn't managed to find him to let him know his wife's remains had been found.

Jill shook her head. 'No, we woke up one day to find a removal van outside and within a couple of hours he and the baby was gone. No longer entitled to an army quarter, what with Hazel gone, like.'

Crane thanked Jill for her help and walked across the garrison to the Welfare Service.

The Army Welfare Services were there to help with: relationship difficulties, bereavement, CSA concerns, parenting skills, childcare, special needs, benefits information, housing debt, equal opportunities issues. In other words, a Citizens Advice service for army personnel.

So, did Hazel visit welfare for help? Likely, if she was having personal and relationship problems. And a screaming baby was a challenge for anyone, Crane was sure, thinking back to when Daniel was a baby and he and Tina had struggled as new parents. They weren't really sure what to do. Crane also wondered if Hazel had been lent on to leave the army because of her personal circumstances. Would that have led to her murder? Or her disappearance, which then turned into her murder?

Whatever the thinking, her file had been left untouched because she'd gone AWOL - or so the authorities thought.

He was woken from his musings by someone he least expected to see on the Garrison, for striding towards him was Diane Chambers. She had been his nemesis whilst working in Aldershot, either in the army or for the police. Always chipping away at cases, wanting more and more information, when there was previous little to give her. It looked as though this might be such an occasion.

'Well, well, well,' she said, 'Who'd have thought it? Sgt Major Crane.'

'Retired.'

'Forgive me. Retired. How the hell are you?'

'Good thank you, Diane, but what are you doing here?'

'Oh you know...' she waved a hand around that contained a smouldering cigarette. Diane was dressed casually with ripped jeans and a blazer over a white t-shirt. Her short dark curls shone in the sunlight and flat leather shoes completed the look. Crane thought she was dressing too young for her age. But then again Diane Chambers never did conform to the expected.

Crane barked a laugh. 'No, I never do know, not with you,

Diane. Or if I do, I wished I didn't. It normally means you're too close to the truth of the matter and exposing it before we can.'

'And now?'

'Sorry?'

'What are you doing on the Garrison and going to pay Welfare a visit if I'm not wrong?'

'Oh you know…' Crane mimicked her words and gesture, minus the cigarette in her hand. He'd given them up when Daniel had been born.

'Hang on,' said Diane 'I thought I saw you a few days ago on the building site, where they found that body. It was you, wasn't it? But I thought Anderson had retired?'

'He has.'

'So…,' Crane could see the cogs working. 'Bloody hell you're helping Billy Williams aren't you? I just did a big piece on the new structure of the military police.'

'Now hang on, Diane.'

'Don't worry, Crane, it will be great working with you again. I'll be in touch,' and off she strode with a grin on her face, leaving Crane with a sinking feeling. He'd hoped he'd dropped off Diane Chamber's radar, but it seemed he had no such luck.

ALDERSHOT NEWS

One of our longest servicing policemen here in Aldershot, is retiring. Detective Inspector Anderson has worked his last days of a 22-year illustrious career.

As Inspector Anderson walked through the precinct one last time, I was lucky enough to accompany him. Imagine the memories that must have flashed through his mind! He remembered his first day on the job, when he was just a rookie, eager to make a difference. He remembered the cases he'd solved, the criminals he'd caught, and the people he'd helped.

But there was one case that stood out above all the rest, one that has haunted him for years. It was the case of the serial killer who had been terrorizing the area for months some 10 years ago now. The killer had been dubbed 'The Shadow' because he always struck at night and left no trace behind.

Anderson had worked tirelessly on the case, analysing every piece of evidence and interviewing every witness. But despite his best efforts, The Shadow remained one step ahead of him. And as he sat there on his final day in the job, Anderson couldn't help but wonder what had become of the killer.

Anderson's retirement will be Aldershot's loss. The recent partnership of Crane and Anderson had closed many cases in the area, and they should be applauded and rewarded for their service to the community.

However, one thing that shouldn't be overlooked is Sgt Major Crane's current situation. Is Crane retiring as well? No one seems to be talking about that, but it's tickled my antenna, so dear readers, I'll keep you posted.

Diane Chambers

Editor Aldershot News

15

Billy was still struggling with the British Army 'zero tolerance' policy on drug use among its soldiers.

Now there were seventeen soldiers, and on top of that, two Sergeants, who faced being discharged from the Army after being caught using performance-enhancing drugs in the Forces' biggest reported case of doping.

Wanting to know who had supplied the drugs and how they had been brought onto the garrison, Billy decided to go and talk to James Clark, one of the Sgt Majors under investigation.

His knock on the army quarter was answered by James himself. A huge, hulk of a man, who seemed to swell before Billy, as he realised who was at his door.

'Fucking hell, it's the Branch. What do you want? I've been advised not to talk to you without representation.'

'Cut the crap, James,' said Billy, who knew the man well. 'Can't we just have a conversation?'

He endured the piercing look of the man who loomed over him.

'Bloody hell, Billy, come on in then. Want a drink?' James tossed over his shoulder. 'I've got a pretty good protein shake.'

'Just a cup of tea, please,' Billy grinned, glad to see his friend hadn't lost his sense of humour.

James led the way into a small kitchen with barely enough room for two people, so Billy stayed at the doorway. After making the tea, James handed Billy the hot mug and said, 'Let's go and sit down.'

Once they were seated at either end of a faded tan leather settee, Billy said, 'Look I might be able to help you here. I need information and if you're willing to help, then I can put in a good word so that you might not be trounced out of the army.'

'You're assuming I want to stay in.'

'James, come on, of course you do. What would you actually do in Civvy street. They don't have much call for parachute specialists at the Job Centre.'

James stroked his ginger beard for a moment. 'What do you want to know?'

'Who supplied the sports supplements?'

'The protein powder?'

Billy nodded.

'Dave Cooper. Local man. He told me it was one thing, and it turned out to be another.'

'So, you were stupid.'

'Yeah,' James had the good grace to hang his head. 'He told us it was clean, didn't he? And I believed him, like a fucking idiot.'

'Is he on the garrison?'

'No, he left, didn't he?'

'Left? Why?'

'Because his missus disappeared, and he had to move out with his kid like.'

'Oh, that Dave Cooper!'

'Why do you say that?' Then the penny dropped. James said, 'Oh God he's the bloke whose wife's remains have just been found.'

Billy nodded. 'It looks like the two cases could be intertwined.'

'Watch Dave Cooper, mind,' James said.

'Really?' Billy looked askance.

'Really. What with the bloody body found and the drugs charges, life is getting a bit hot for him. He's already leaned on the men not to reveal him as their source. Of the drugs, you know.'

'So why have you just given me his name?'

'Because I don't like being threatened by an arsehole. I told him I'd cut him another one if he came round threatening me again. At which point he turned and fled,' James laughed.

16

Crane was still trying to speak to any neighbours of Hazel and Dave Cooper that he could find.

He wished there was CCTV footage of the couple, but that was a bust. It was simply too long ago. However, Crane managed to speak to a neighbour who had lived opposite the Coopers. The woman, Jo Lake, told him pretty much what he knew already. That there was a lot of strain in the relationship and the baby became very unhappy as a result. Then Jo said, 'Hazel mentioned a brother at one point.'

'Really?' said Crane his interest finally piqued.

'Yes. Step-brother, I think. I asked Hazel if she saw much of him, and said she hoped not, he was a bully who was too handy with his fists. Hazel had wondered what was wrong with her, seeing as she thought she brought out the worst in men. I told her not to be so stupid,' Jo continued. 'It wasn't her fault some men were like that. But I did warn her that if things were that bad, it was a good idea to take herself out of the equation and scarper.

'But then something strange happened. A man was banging on the Cooper's door. I went out and asked him what the hell he thought he was doing. He said he was looking for his sister and gave me a name I didn't recognise. It certainly wasn't the name of my neighbour. So, I told him there was no such person here and to go away otherwise I'd call the military police. At that he buggered off sharpish.'

'Did you tell her what had happened, when you next saw her?'

'I meant to, but to be honest I forgot and then when I remembered I didn't want to upset her, so I stayed quiet.'

'Did you ever see him again?'

Jo nodded and bit her lip.

'When?'

'A few days before she disappeared… I've often wondered if I'd done the wrong thing by not telling her.'

Crane did as well but kept that thought to himself. 'Can you remember the name he gave you?' he asked her.

'Um, it was still Hazel, but the surname was different.'

'Could you try and remember, this could be important.'

'Oh, I don't know. I think it was something to do with the time of year, Autumn maybe? Winter? No, I'm just not sure enough, sorry. It was some time ago now.'

'Any chance you can remember what he looked like?'

'Didn't see much of his face, he had a cap pulled down over it, you know? And his clothing was dark. Jeans and hoodie. Pretty generic I'm afraid.'

Crane realised that was as much as he was going to get from her. And after all it was three years ago since she'd seen someone purporting to be Hazel's brother.

'Thank you for your time, Mrs Lake. And if you think of anything else…' Crane handed her a card.

'Yes, of course,' and Jo Lake retreated into her house, closing the door firmly on Crane, who sighed. Jo Lake could be right, he thought. Hazel Cooper might still be alive if Jo Lake had warned her that her brother was about looking for her. Or whatever the hell he was to her.

But it was best not to jump to conclusions. He needed evidence, not rumour and hearsay and it was up to him to get it.

17

Crane realised he had to speak again to Hazel's mother, Cora Young, who lived up in Newcastle. But this time he did a video call rather than resort to an aeroplane again.

'Morning, Cora, thank you for taking the time to speak to me.'

'You're like a bad penny, son, so you are. I guessed that if I didn't speak to you now, you'd just harass me until a did.'

Crane smiled in reply. Cora Young was spot on there. 'So, I wanted to ask you if you had a son?'

Cora Young frowned. 'No. Why?'

'Because someone purporting to be Hazel's brother was seen banging on her front door, down here on Aldershot Garrison, just before she died.'

Cora Young paled so much that Crane could see it on the monitor. It was more a draining of the blood in her face, being replaced by ice in her veins. Crane knew he had to push her. The information could be vital to his investigation.

'Cora? What is it?'

'She, she, has, sorry had, like, a half-brother.'

'A half-brother?'

'Yes, that's what I said,' she snapped. But then gave Crane the information he required. 'My husband, her father, was married before and had a boy by that marriage. But we don't have anything to do with him, as he blames me and Hazel for splitting up his family.'

'How? Why?'

'Because his dad and me were having an affair, like, and when I got pregnant his father left his wife and the boy, for me.'

'I see. How do I get in touch with him?'

Cora Young disappeared from the screen and when she came back, she had an address and phone number.

'I don't know how current this is, but it's the only information I have. I've no one left now. I'm all on my own. Maybe that's why his lad has left me alone. To suffer, you know?'

'Do you think he might have harmed Hazel? And somehow killed your husband?'

I wouldn't put it past him. In fact, I'd say it's definitely a possibility.'

After they'd finished their call, Cora's words rang in Crane's ears… Maybe that's why his lad has left me alone. To suffer. She could well be right. He decided that it was tragic what families did to each other over a slight. Real or imagined.

18

Billy was sat around the table with his officer commanding, Major Rhodes and the equivalent officer from the Parachute Regiment, Major Dunston.

'So, what's the verdict, Billy?' Major Rhodes asked. 'What are your conclusions from the investigation.' Rhodes looked exhausted. Billy could see new wrinkles appearing on his face and neck as he lost weight. His pallor seemed greyer than normal and he'd aged over the three months Billy had known him. It seemed the stress of the tri-service arrangements was getting to Rhodes.

'They are bloody idiots,' replied Billy, meaning every word of his blunt statement.

'Really?'

'Really, Sir. It wasn't an intentional bending of the drugs rules by taking steroids, by all accounts. They were misinformed, mislead, call it what you will. They had a supplier who convinced them that the powders were clean. But, of course, they weren't. So, as I said, if they're guilty of anything, it's being bloody stupid and not doing their own due diligence.'

'Who was the supplier?' asked Dunston. By contrast Dunston was looking particularly chipper, even in the light of the drugs scandal.

'A chap called Dave Cooper. He used to live on Aldershot garrison, back in the day, which is how they know him. His wife was in the army. But then she disappeared a few years ago.'

'Are you talking about the body recovered last month? Was that his wife?' asked Rhodes.

'Yes, Sir. We're trying to trace him in connection with that. And now, of course, in connection with the sale of the powder as well.'

'So, where do we go from here? Bearing in mind that the army have a zero tolerance with regard to drugs,' Dunston wanted to know.

'I understand that, Sir. But we're not talking about cocaine, or even weed. We're talking about the innocent ingestion of body building protein powder, which contained a banned substance.'

Rhodes thought for a moment, then said, 'How about the argument that zero tolerance is all very well, but is it really necessary to lose so many experienced soldiers?'

'Especially as it was a case of being duped, rather than purposefully taking steroids.'

'If we believe the soldiers,' growled Dunston.

'Yes, sir, which is one of the reasons why we're trying to trace Dave Cooper.'

'I know, I know,' replied Rhodes. 'The regimental Commanding Officer is now weighing up the cost of losing 17 soldiers against his obligation to the Army's 'zero-tolerance' drugs policy. In exceptional circumstances, a commanding officer may choose a more lenient punishment and remedial training.'

'Let's hope he sees this as exceptional circumstances,' muttered Billy as he was dismissed from the meeting. For in his eyes losing so many trained soldiers would be unjust. He understood dismissal for a coke habit, or God forbid, worse. But this? Billy believed they were guilty of being bloody stupid. He'd just have to do all he could to make the powers that be practice leniency.

19

After the conversation with Hazel's mother, Crane realised that he had to find two people.

Hazel Winter's stepbrother Arthur Young, as well as Hazel Cooper's husband, Dave Cooper. He picked up the file with Hazel's post-mortem results in it and read it for the umpteenth time. Nowhere contained in that were any clues that might help him. So, if there was nothing the body could tell him, he needed to turn his attention to any forensic evidence.

Asking Bob Hunt for the items taken from Hazel Cooper's shallow grave once again, he removed the lid of the plastic storage box everything was kept in. Each item was in its own bag, marked with the date and time of finding, and including signatures of everyone who had handled the items.

There was the handbag that Crane had looked at before and was certain there was nothing more it could tell him. There were various items of jewellery none of note, none silver or gold, apart from her wedding ring, which was a plain gold band. Finally, there was a pillowcase that was found over the head of the body. Parts of it had rotted away, but there was still a good deal of it left.

Crane pondered. Who would have put a pillowcase over the head of the body? The killer. Why? Guilt? He couldn't face what he'd done to her. So, he'd covered her. Hid the effects of his actions. She would have looked pretty horrific, Crane realised. Strangulation wasn't quite as bad as a hanging, but her eyes would still have bulged, and her tongue swollen.

It was also possible that she'd been lying on the pillow when she'd been strangled. Therefore, there could be DNA present on it, not just from the victim, but possibly from her attacker. Walking over to Hunt, he asked about the testing on the pillowcase.

'None was found, other than the victims,' Crane was assured.

'Can you try again?'

'Why?' Hunt asked, but his tone suggested he was asking out of curiosity rather than anger.

'Because there could be DNA on it from the killer. He could have dripped sweat onto it. Touched it with sweaty hands. He had to get it over her head somehow, which means he touched it either before she died, or after.'

'Seriously?'

'Very. If we don't try everything that we can possibly do, then we're letting our victim down. She deserves justice. What if it was your wife? Your daughter? Your mother? You'd want every little thing done, wouldn't you?'

'Alright,' Hunt grinned. 'Give it here. I'll do it next.'

Crane turned away to hide the sardonic smile that was playing across his face. That little speech was always effective in bringing out the best in people.

The next day the results were in. The forensic duo had found unknown DNA on the pillowcase. However, there was no match in the database. Maybe if he found Hazel's illusive stepbrother it might be a match to him.

And so, the hunt for Arthur Young, continued.

20

Diane Chambers, of course, had reported on the death of Hazel Cooper.

She was a former soldier who had died and her body found on the edge of the garrison near to where the latest building work was being carried out. She was still digging into the death. She'd been on the barracks, seen the site of the burial and was now writing the copy. Looking at the screen of the laptop she sighed. It was very boring, if she was honest. She could flower up her copy, but it would only be stuffing and that wasn't her style.

She had to find the dead woman's husband. She rang a couple of policemen she knew and an informant, Nuts, who regularly helped with information she needed for the paper. Infact he was the one who came through. The police either didn't know anything or were not talking.

She met Nuts outside the Aldershot football ground, as fans were streaming in through the turnstiles. She was stood looking at the match board, when Nuts approached her. He was wearing his trademark Aldershot football shirt with a bucket hat on his head. Jeans and trainers completed the look. Diane wasn't sure what style he was aiming for, but whatever it was, he'd clearly missed the mark. Anyways, he slipped her a piece of paper and she passed him a tenner. Nuts went into the ground with a grin on his face being £10 up on the day, and she melted away towards the town centre.

Diane stopped at the first café she came to and ordered a coffee. Sat in the window she looked at the paper Nuts had given her. It contained the name of a local pub.

Don't know his address, Nuts had written. But he drinks in

this pub most nights.

Diane checked her diary, she was free that night, so she might just pop in for a dink after work.

It was gone 6pm when she turned up at The Crimea. She hadn't been in the pub for years but from what she could remember, it hadn't changed much, apart from to look tired. It was clean enough she had to admit but was badly in need of a redecoration.

Taking her gin and tonic she wandered over to an empty table. She only had to wait 10 minutes before Dave Cooper walked it. At least she thought that's who he was. He was pretty much the same as Nuts had described him. He got a pint and stayed standing at the bar chatting to someone who was clearly a mate. When his friend went to the loo, she moved in.

At the bar she stood behind him, then tipped up her glass and said, 'Excuse me, but could you watch your elbows.'

'Eh?' he said, turning to look at her. 'Your elbow, my glass,' she said as she picked it up off the bar. 'Well, isn't it Dave Cooper?' she asked. 'Sorry I was just thinking of you. And there you were!'

'What? Who the hell are you?'

'Diane Chambers, Editor of the Aldershot News.'

'Well, why don't you fuck off, Diane Chambers, Editor of the Aldershot News, I've nothing to say to you.'

'But…'

'But nothing. Do as you're told and leave. Now.'

As he glowered at her and bunched his fist, she decided that leaving Dave Cooper alone was probably the best move. Gathering what was left of her pride, she left Dave Cooper alone by leaving. As she left, she felt his eyes on the back of her neck.

Once outside she turned left, walking down the street and trying not to run. Determine to try and save some of her dignity.

21

Crane decided to take a walk while he mulled over what he knew.

He'd just entered Ash Ranges, when saw her—Jean Wilder. A vision from his past, from a previous case with Anderson.

She hadn't noticed him yet, as her focus was on her little dog. She swung her long black hair so like his dead wife, Tina's, over her shoulder. He caught a glimpse of green eyes that twinkled, full lips and a smile to die for. Casually dressed in jeans and t shirt she came striding towards Crane.

He couldn't help but smile at the sight of her and decided to ask if she'd like to go for a cup of coffee. When asked what he was doing, Crane was hesitant to tell her about his cold case involving bodies yet could feel the words slipping out.

She burst out laughing and commented 'What is it with you and buried bodies, Crane?'

As they settled down at a table in the nearest pub with their coffees, he teased, 'Seen any more dead ghosts in your house? Or has Lucky here found any more bones?'

The thought of dead bodies in her garden had freaked her out last year, he knew. Especially as her granddaughter had seen an old couple walk through a wall. Jean herself found them in her kitchen and then her dog refused to go into a very cold bedroom. But she'd been determined not to leave, and it had been the right decision, she said. Crane was glad for her. Everyone needed to get to a place where they were settled and happy and felt safe, as he knew only too well. He wasn't quite there yet, he still had a ways to go.

The two spent a very pleasant hour catching up and chatting, before Crane shyly suggested they have dinner one night. To his surprise, she agreed at once, and they made arrangements for later in the week.

As they embraced as they left, Jean's pale skin was soft and smooth to the touch. Her hands soft as a whisper on Crane's face, her lips soft and full, her breath a hint of peppermint coffee as she pecked a kiss on his cheek. They exchanged mobile numbers before saying goodbye.

As she climbed into her car, Crane realised he hadn't done what he'd intended to do. Think over the case, but for once didn't mind. He'd just been reminded that there was more to life than work and that was a road he was happy to travel down.

But the work wouldn't go away and so Crane settled in his car and pulled out his mobile, for he needed to speak to Hazel's mother. Again.

His call was answered with the words 'For god's sake, not you again.'

'Sorry, Mrs Young but I need everything you have on your husband's first family.'

'I don't know any more than I told you,' she grumbled.

'Is there nothing you can look at, papers you can check? Diaries?' Crane insisted.

She laughed. 'Bert wasn't one for writing stuff, not even a shopping list. But there is a box in the loft. If someone can climb up and get it you can have it. It was his, I've no idea what's in it, he brought it with him when he moved in and it's been there all these years. Couldn't bring myself to open it when he passed – you know?'

'Indeed I do, Mrs Young.'

Crane felt his leg twinge at the thought of a climb into a loft, but at least he wouldn't have to do that. He'd send someone to the house to climb into the loft and find the box then have it sent straight down to Aldershot, without opening it of course.

HAZEL FIVE
YEARS AGO

And then she met Dave Cooper.

It was one night, while out with mates from the unit in The Crimea. He was holding court in the pub, telling funny stories and making suggestive comments. He caught her eye and gestured if she'd like a drink. Never one to turn down free alcohol. She nodded her thanks and when he brought the drinks over, she sat with him at a free table.

'Cheers,' he said raising his glass.

'Cheers,' she replied. 'I'm Hazel.'

'And I'm Dave.'

And that was the start of it. A whirl-wind romance ensued. He was larger than life, which is what she liked about him. The test came when she was going away for three months.

'Will you wait for me?' she asked.

He looked askance. 'Why wouldn't I?'

'Perhaps a truer statement would be, why would you?'

'Is that what you think of me?' he asked pacing across the window of his flat. 'That I'm so shallow?'

'Yes...no... of course not.'

'In that case I'll just have to prove to you that I'm committed to this relationship.'

'Prove to me?'

'Oh yes,' she grinned, standing up. 'How?'

'If I wait for you...'

'Yes?' she prompted.

'Then we'll get married.'

'Oh my God, oh my God,' she squeaked. 'Are you sure?'

'Of course I am, come here you silly moo.'

And so Hazel melted into his arms, feeling that at last she'd met her Prince Charming.

22

It was only two days later that Crane had his hands on the box.

They tingled as he anticipated going through the contents and the secrets that might be contained in it. He hoped to God he could get some answers.

Looking at the ragged cardboard box, Crane wondered if the good stuff would be at the bottom, i.e. earliest documents, with newer ones on top, thrown in as the years went by. So he went for it and tipped the box upside down on his desk. Managing to keep the papers from falling all over the floor, he grabbed a couple of random pieces.

For some reason Bert had the birth certificates of his three children (including Crane's missing person). According to the box he had two male children from his first marriage Reece and Arthur Young. Which one was after Hazel?

Delving deeper in the box he found a committal certificate for Arthur. It seemed he'd spent several months in a clinic while he dried out from an excess of alcohol and drugs, particularly cocaine. It was noted that he had a violent temper, which could burst forth at any moment, induced or otherwise. What had that incarceration done for Arthur? Had it been successful? But the box didn't give Crane any clues for the moment.

Next out of the box was a newspaper cutting that told how Reece had been in a car accident, a hit and run, and had died from his injuries. There was talk about Reece being drunk and weaving off the pavement into the path of the oncoming car, but the article dismissed that as speculation. Reece had been a gardener and was working on the driveway of a large, local manor house. He'd begun his walk home when the driver, failing to spot Reece, hit him, throwing the body into a ditch at the side of the road, filled with water. By the time the emergency services reached him, he had died from his injuries.

Therefore, the only remaining stepbrother would be Arthur, who was more than likely unstable, if he had once more succumbed to the lure of alcohol and drugs. Was he the one who hated his father's second family for taking him away from them? But killed his stepsister, rather than her mother, his stepmother, as he wanted her to feel what he did – the pain and loss of family?

Who knew, but it was a good lead for Crane to follow up. That gave Crane a pool of suspects, including Hazel's stepbrother, and her abusive husband. Or even someone else? He couldn't rule out the possibility of her killer being a fellow soldier, because, if you think about it, a squaddie would be the one who knew where to bury her.

But so far there was nothing to suggest a man fixated on Hazel. Accessing the military police database giving details of the cases worked the year Hazel died, he found that there were no complaints by Hazel about fellow soldiers and no reports of fighting. Looking like that was a bust, the next thing Crane had to do was to check with Welfare about any domestic problems she might have been having.

But that was for another day, as Crane had a very important engagement that night.

23

It was time for Det Inspector Anderson to retire.

He had to face facts. He wasn't as young as he used to be. He'd finished work last week and this party was to be his last official duty.

He looked around the crowded, noisy private function room at a local hotel. He was surrounded by familiar faces, some he'd known for years, others were more recent acquaintances. Either way, all were colleagues who had come to see him off on his retirement journey. The laughter of old stories mixed with reminisces were like music to his ears, yet he could feel a wave of sadness wash over him. This was it—the end of an era for him and the start of a new chapter for him and Jean.

The evening had seemed a fitting way to show that he was passing the torch to a new generation of police officers. The younger men would toil while he took his pension and hobbled down to give the occasional lecture at the Police Academy on good investigation techniques. He could feel the frozen aches of arthritis slapping him from inside his bones, but when you were born into a life of being tough, it was hard to leave it behind.

His friends and colleagues offered words of encouragement, but there was an air of regret. Through sheer willpower, he managed to smile and enjoy himself, despite the sadness of saying farewell.

When another drink was pressed into his hand, he looked up and saw Crane. With a woman? Really? And then it tumbled into place. Where he'd seen her before.

'Mrs Wilder, how lovely to see you. I hope Crane here is looking after you.'

Goodness knows how Crane had persuaded her to come. Or even why. He was saved by his wife navigating the choppy waters of social etiquette and with a smooth manoeuvre, steered Jean Wilder away out of earshot.

'Evening, Anderson,' Crane said. 'Enjoying your do?'

'Yes, thanks,' he dismissed the question, 'Mrs Wilder? How? When? Where?'

That made Crane laugh. 'We ran into each other at Ash Ranges the other week.'

'Well, you kept that quiet.'

'Do you blame me? I didn't fancy the Spanish Inquisition.'

Anderson spluttered a laugh into his drink. After wiping his mouth with a handkerchief, he said, 'Fair enough. So, are you going to tell me about it?'

'No, sorry,' said Crane and buggered off before Anderson could try again.

He found Jean easily enough, standing with Anderson's wife, gazing past her shoulder and looking at him. Her eyes were swimming with tears. He frowned. What on earth could be the matter?

As Anderson's wife peeled away, Crane swept around and met Jean Wilder by her side.

'Having a nice time?' he asked. 'What were you talking to Jean Anderson about?'

Mrs Wilder turned to Crane, putting her drink on a side table. 'I'd like to go home, please,' she said. 'Will you take me, or shall I call a taxi?'

'Jean… What…? Of course, I'll take you home, if that's what you really want to do.'

'Yes, please. Thank you.'

Once they were settled in the car, it was only a short journey to Jean Wilder's house, but quite a long walk in the wind and rain. Neither had spoken.

Once he'd stopped the car outside her home, he said, 'Before you go, could you tell me what the matter is?'

'Tina,' Jean said, the name sending a cold shiver down Crane's back.

'What on earth? Tina? But she's dead,' he stuttered, not understanding the problem.

'She might as well be bloody alive, the way you feel about her.'

'Oh.' That was all Crane could manage, struggling not to be drawn back into the emotional pain of Tina's passing.

'I had an interesting talk with Mrs Anderson,' Jean said. 'She told me all about Tina's death and your dogged investigation to find that man who liked to hear people die on the phone. She told me how much in love you two were and how happy you both were when Tina discovered she was pregnant.'

'Oh,' said Crane again, a small sound, drowned out by the sadness prevalent in the car.

'I won't be second best to anyone,' she said.

'B b but,' Crane stammered.

'Look, Crane, I'm not sure you are over your wife's death. The Andersons certainly don't think so. I'd like you to think long and hard about me, Tina and you. Let me know if you can find a way forward that doesn't include the ghost of Tina. I'm sorry, Tom, but maybe you'll understand more if I tell you that at the moment there are three of us in this relationship and it's getting rather crowded.'

With that Jean Wilder got out of Tom's car and ran for the house, her handbag held over her head to stave off the wind and rain.

Crane should go back to the Retirement Party, but he felt hollowed out. Not sure what to do for the best. He had tried his best to keep Tina alive for Daniel, but maybe he was going too far down that road. Daniel deserved to come to terms with Tina's death, as did Crane. He was beginning to feel fed up of a half-life in Tina's shadow.

Jean Wilder had shown him a different way to live. And been absolutely right when she intimated there were three of them in their relationship, instead of two. Crane had to choose between the two women in his life and as far as Jean Wilder was concerned, Crane didn't think he had a lot of time to make that decision.

24

Crane eased the car off the drive and glanced at Daniel, sitting on his booster seat in the back.

'Okay kiddo?' he asked.

'Yes, dad,' he managed to mumble around his thumb, his attention firmly on the small screen on the back of the front passenger seat. Crane knew it was a cop out, both letting him suck his thumb and watching cartoons, but sometimes needs must and it would mean a quiet 30 minute run to Daniel's grandparents. Daniel loved going to see them and Crane was pleased that they had all managed to maintain their relationship since their only daughter died, for the sake of the little boy.

'Yeah!' Daniel cheered as Crane pulled up outside the house and he scrambled to open his car door.

'Hey, not so fast,' chided Crane. 'I'll come round and let you out.'

As soon as Daniel's feet hit the ground he was off running. 'Nanny!' he shouted and the smile his grandmother gave him was just so lovely to see. She knelt down and caught him in a hug. Looking over the boy's shoulder, she mouthed a thank you to Crane.

Moving at a slower pace, Crane grabbed Daniel's bag and went to give it to the boy.

'Do come in, Tom,' she invited. 'I've got some coffee on the go.'

'Sorry, Martha. I've got to get back for a meeting with Padre Symmonds. Saturday morning was the only time he was free. But I tell you what, I'll stay and catch up when I pick Daniel up tomorrow.'

Martha nodded, 'Yes, do, Tom, we'll look forward to it.

After kissing both Daniel and his grandmother, Crane returned to the car, buckled up and turned around, nose pointing back to Aldershot.

The meeting with Padre Symmonds was both to catch up on his private life and to talk to him about providing a burial service for Hazel.

Once at the Garrison Church, Crane followed the smell of freshly brewed coffee to Symmond's office at the back of the building. He was greeted warmly by the Padre and managed to find a spare chair to sit on. Both men were dressed down in civvies, arguably shopping from the same store, their chinos and polo shirts being almost identical.

'Thanks for seeing me, Padre,' began Crane.

'Of course,' murmured Symmonds, 'anytime. So, was there anything in particular you wanted to discuss?'

'Yes, it's the remains of Hazel Cooper. Could we arrange a quiet burial, do you think?'

'Ah, so forensics have finished their investigation, I take it?'

'Yes. But the problem is I can't find her husband and her mother lives all the way up in Newcastle, so I was thinking that perhaps... as she was army...'

'How about just an internment,' said the Padre.

'What's just an internment?'

'Similar to when ashes are placed in the ground at a suitable location. The military section of the graveyard here, for instance. As I understand it we don't have the full skeleton and I think a coffin would be excessive, as would a cremation. So as an alternative, I would just bless the remains and then they would be placed in the ground. What do you think?'

'I think that's ideal, Padre, thank you very much. I just feel that Hazel deserves some sort of ceremony to mark her passing.'

'Let me see,' the Padre opened his diary. 'I could do it Monday 15th, just over two weeks' time. Say, 10 am?'

Crane nodded his agreement as the Padre made the entry in his diary.

'Now onto pleasanter things,' declared Symmonds. 'Tell

me, who was that glamorous woman on your arm at Derek's retirement party?'

Crane was sure he blushed, as he cast about for anything else to talk about, rather than Jean Wilder. 'Just a friend,' he managed to mumble.

'Mmm,' said the Padre. 'Just good friends, that old chestnut, eh?'

'Well, I'm afraid that's all you're going to get,' grinned Crane. 'Now, tell me all about Billy. Is he still with the prison governor?'

'Yes, they have a married quarter on the garrison.'

'Married? How come I wasn't invited?'

'None of us were. A drunken night in Las Vega by all accounts.'

Crane roared with laughter.

'Anyway, Emma is good friends with Kim. Emma is thinking of training with Kim to become a counsellor. So, it will be similar to what she did in the Prison Service, but a damn sight safer.'

Crane nodded his agreement. He remembered when Emma was working for the prison service in Reading and had various crimes to investigate, some of which involved Billy.

'Well good luck to them both,' Crane said, hoping they would be able to keep their marriage on course. Being married in the Army wasn't very comfortable at times, as a soldier was married to the army first and the wife, second.

25

Despite the nuggets of information about the two boys, there was no paperwork relating to Hazel in the box.

He'd waded through Xmas cards, till receipts, product flyers and the odd letter, only to find there was nothing else of value in the cardboard box. Crane believed anything relating to Hazel must have gone with her, when she married Winter.

So, what to do? He decided a visit to Welfare was in order.

Doing Welfare Duty was a Sergeant Storey and Crane found him in his office, leafing through files.

'Morning, Sergeant,' Crane announced himself to the man at the desk, who looked very familiar.

'Sir,' said Storey as he stood. 'How can I help you?'

It was hearing his voice that did it. 'Well, I never, Steve Storey. For God's sake, man, sit down,' said Crane, 'I'm too long out of the army to be bothered with all that.'

'Yes, sir, thank you sir,' said Storey and did as Crane asked. 'How can I help you?'

Crane told his tale of Hazel Cooper's remains being found, her husband in the wind and no paperwork to speak of. 'And therefore, I need your help. I need any Welfare records for Hazel and Dave Cooper. Please. It would help a great deal.'

'Well, without a search warrant...' Storey said.

'I know that, man, but she's dead, so are they still confidential records? Listen, Steve,' Crane edged closer to his desk. 'I just want to find her killer and get justice for Hazel. She was one of us, after all.'

Storey stared at Crane, then said, 'Alright,' and he picked up the telephone, asking for anything on Hazel Cooper, or her husband, and to copy it and bring it in for Crane, alongside a coffee. 'The good stuff,' he ordered.

After chewing the fat for a few minutes, the files were brought in, along with the enticing aroma of coffee beans. As Crane flipped through the file, he saw she had been living with her partner for several years after she got the quarter. According to their records, her partner was confirmed as Dave Cooper. He was known to be abusive as he had laid his hands on her once. But after she floored him in unarmed combat, he'd never tried anything like that again. So she said. But was that the truth? Who knew what went on behind closed doors?

Crane wondered whether Cooper had been so upset by being humiliated by his woman, that he wanted to show her who was boss. Was that why she was killed? Cooper would have had plenty of chance to smother her, or strangle her, if he caught her unawares, or if she was ill and vulnerable. But without being able to interview the man, all he was doing was guessing. What he needed was either hard evidence, or a confession.

26

Billy looked at the drugs file, one more time.

The charge was that the soldiers, who followed an arduous physical training regime, were understood to have claimed that they took the ephedrine - an ingredient in a type of bodybuilding product called 'fat stripper' – unwittingly. Available legally as prescription medicine, it was also contained in unlicensed sports supplements sold online.

According to his report, Captain Johnson couldn't believe what he had heard. His soldiers, the ones he'd trusted with his life, had been taking illicit substances to enhance their performance.

At a meeting with the soldiers responsible for this drug scandal, Johnson reported that they looked sheepish and apologetic. Johnson knew he had to be firm but fair in his handling of the situation. He asked them to explain why they resorted to taking ephedrine.

One soldier spoke up. 'Sir, we didn't know it was illegal. We thought it was just a harmless supplement to help us with our bodybuilding goals. We never thought it would get us into trouble.'

Johnson had known that this was a common excuse, but he also knew that he needed to be understanding and tackle the root cause of the problem. He issued a stern warning to them. You all know the rules,' he said sternly. 'No illegal substances, no unlicensed supplements. We have a code of conduct to uphold, and you have all broken it.' But he also knew that these were his soldiers, his team, and he needed to help them if he could.

'And so, Sgt Williams,' he had written, 'is there any way to safe my soldiers from themselves? I know they've done wrong, and so do they, but shouldn't they be given the chance to make recompense? In the modern army perhaps we need to be more flexible than in the past.'

27

The next morning when Crane entered the office, he found a file waiting for him on his desk.

'Morning, Crane,' called Dudley-Jones.

Crane sauntered over to see him.

'I had a few minutes last night, so ran Alex Winter for you, deceased ex-husband of Hazel Winter.

'Deceased?'

'Yep, he's dead. Full details in the file on your desk.'

'Cheers, Dudley-Jones. Has anyone told you you're the best?'

'Frequently. Now piss off and let me get on, take your cheeriness somewhere else.'

As Crane turned away, Dudley-Jones called, 'Hang on a minute, Crane. Cheery? What the hell? What's going on with you, I didn't think cheery was in your character. Or even a word in your vocabulary!'

'Live and learn, Dudley-Jones,' said Crane as he grinned and walked away.

It was true, Crane was becoming less curmudgeonly in his demeanour, starting to find pleasure in things. Well, if he was honest, starting to like Jean Wilder. But what Dudley-Jones had just said was a warning. Crane couldn't become too nice at work, otherwise no one would do anything for him. He made a note to self to stop being so bloody cheerful, at least on the outside, if not the inside.

Grabbing a coffee from the kitchen, Crane returned to his desk and opened the file. He read how Alex Winter was found dead in a hostel where he was staying, after he'd done a spell inside for an unrelated incident. Blunt force trauma to the head. Someone must have hated him, as it was a frenzied attack.

As Crane examined the crime scene photographs, he could see the room was a mess, with clothes and belongings scattered all over the floor. Crane's eyes wandered around the room, trying to find something that would explain what happened. he noticed a large, bloodstained object lying on the floor near the bed. It looked like a rock or a brick that had been used to bludgeon Winter to death.

Crane's mind raced with questions. Who had done this to him? Was it someone he knew? And why had no one said anything? He knew that most people in the hostel wouldn't want to draw attention to themselves, but surely someone must have seen or heard something. Was his death anything to do with his ex-partner, Hazel?

He turned to the results of the post-mortem, but that didn't offer any more clues. As Crane delved deeper into the file, he discovered that Alex had been released from prison just two days before his death. He had been serving time for possession of drugs, but Crane couldn't help but wonder if there was more to his sentence than met the eye.

28

Crane was on the school run.

Not for Daniel, but to find Hazel Cooper's neighbours once again and pump them for information. Or try to, at least.

'Morning, ladies,' he called over a blustery wind, to a group of mums he recognised.

'Bloody hell,' grumbled one who Crane recalled was Shona.

'Not you again,' piped up Tara.

'Morning, Crane,' said Jodi, the one whose husband was of the highest rank. 'What do you want now?'

At last, someone was pleased to see him, Crane thought. Or if not pleased, at least had a modicum of good manners.

'Sorry, all, but I really need to talk to you about Hazel Cooper one more time.

'What is it this time?' grumbled Tara. 'Hurry up I've got thing to do.'

'Last time we spoke one of you remembered someone coming to the neighbourhood and asking about Hazel.'

'So?'

'So do anyone of you remember that and remember what he looked like?'

'There was someone,' said Jodi, the most helpful of the wives. 'Wanted to know where Hazel was. I told him she was away on exercise, just so he'd leave her alone. He was a tall man, wearing a black hoodie and jeans,' she said, recalling the encounter. 'I couldn't see his face clearly, but he looked familiar.'

'Familiar?'

'Yeah, as though he was wearing a disguise. I don't know. To make himself smaller or less obvious, or summat.' The woman pondered her reply. 'That's it, that's who he reminded me of.'

'Who?' they all asked. 'What are you talking about?'

'He reminded me of Dave Cooper.'

'What? Her husband?' Crane said.

'Yeah. The voice was the same. Gravelly like, you know?' said Jodi.

'Where is he?' one of them asked. 'The bloke who was after Hazel?'

'Dead, we think,' replied Crane bluntly.

'So, it wasn't her husband? Dave Cooper ain't dead I only saw him last week in Budgens,' laughed Tara.

'No, it was her ex-husband by the name of Winter, I think from your description. And he was found dead up North,' Crane clarified.

The neighbours exchanged worried glances. 'Are we in danger?' Jodi asked and drew her baby closer to her chest in its carrier.

'It sounds like Winter's past had caught up with her,' said Tara. 'We'd heard rumours about her ex-husband being a notorious criminal who had disappeared after a police raid.'

'Some said he was dead,' said Tara.

'Others believed he had gone into hiding.'

'No, you're safe, ladies. He is definitely dead. Look, I won't keep you. Thanks for your time.'

As Crane walked away, he fancied he heard the gossip mill springing to life. By mid-morning it would be all over the Garrison. He didn't mind that. It might even draw out someone with something relevant to say.

ALDERSHOT NEWS

This paper understands that the latest military drug test results, timed to coincide with the end of the summer break, spread like wildfire throughout the Aldershot community, causing a stir among soldiers and officers alike. Everyone has been shocked by the number of fails, and rumours have begun to circulate about what really happened.

Last night a regimental source said the drugs test results had shocked all the members of 11 Para RHA. He said: 'We expected maybe five or six fails. That's pretty standard, especially when they test us straight after Christmas or summer leave. But 17 is off the charts, and for a pair of sergeants to get done too, is unheard of.

'But these guys are gym rats rather than recreational drug users, and they're guilty of being stupid for not checking what was in the fat-stripper product, but that's all.'

Our military source, who had just returned from leave, heard the news and was immediately apprehensive. As he walked past the barracks, he overheard soldiers talking about the recent drug test failures. They were discussing how the two sergeants had failed, and how they were surprised that so many others had too.

This paper understands that many soldiers are feeling uneasy about the situation. Many of them have always been clean, never involved in any sort of drug use or abuse. But there would always be a hard core of fellow soldiers that weren't as disciplined. And in the meantime, the cloud of suspicion coats the Garrison like a cloak.

29

After grabbing coffees, Crane met Billy in his office for a discussion on Hazel Cooper's case.

'So, come on, Crane, you mut have an inkling about who it might be. Her stepbrother or ex husband, Dave Cooper?'

Billy was right, for a while Crane had considered Winter. 'It can't be Winter,' he said. 'We now know he was dead before she was, after finding the Death Certificate. That was the end of him, in more words than one. And either way Hazel was still a victim. I wonder, what makes a woman repeat the mistakes of the past,' Crane mused.

Billy leaned back in his chair, sipping on his coffee as he mulled over Hazel's situation. It was clear that she had been through a lot, but Crane was right, why did she keep falling for the same type of man.

'I think it's easy for people to fall back into old patterns, especially if they haven't dealt with the underlying issues,' he said thoughtfully.

'You mean like unresolved trauma?' Crane asked, intrigued.

'Exactly. If a woman has experienced abuse or neglect in the past, she may be drawn to men who exhibit similar characteristics, because it's familiar to her. It's what she knows, and it can be difficult to break the cycle.'

Crane nodded his understanding. 'But what about therapy? Couldn't that have helped her overcome those issues?'

'Sure, therapy can be helpful, but it's not a one-size-fits-all solution. It takes a lot of work and self-reflection to break those patterns. And even then, there are no guarantees. The trouble with Hazel was fear. Fear of being alone, fear of not being loved. Fear of not belonging. Sometimes it's easier to go back to what's familiar, even if it's toxic. Rather than stand on your own two feet.'

'Take responsibility for your own life and make your own decisions.'

'Exactly,' agreed Billy.

'So, what on earth possessed her to join the army?'

'Good question, Crane. I reckon it was because there would always be people telling her what to do. She didn't need independent thinking. She was provided with everything she needed to live, money, food, a roof over her head. See?'

'Yes,' nodded Crane. 'It all too clear now, isn't it. Looking back at her life as a whole. Anyway, it's my job to find her killer, not to psychoanalyse her.

'Yes, but understanding her in some regard, can help you. Don't you think?'

Crane had to agree with Billy. But really what he needed were hard facts, not just theories.

HAZEL THREE
YEARS AGO

It was insidious, how the control and coercion had given way to domestic violence.

Dave was getting worse in his responses, and his behaviour, towards her. If he thought she'd done the tiniest of transgressions, she was likely to get hit, punched or stamped on.

He'd hated her going away on exercise, so he took away her control over her own body, by taking away her contraceptive pills. If she got new ones, he found her hiding places. And so, in time she fell pregnant and before she knew it, she was stuck in a desk job at work and then stuck at home with a baby.

She didn't know if Dave had a history of abusing his girlfriends, but what he did have was raging jealousy issues. When he was being handy with his fists, she often wondered if he would end up killing her in a fit of rage.

The core of domestic violence is power and control, she was told by a charity she'd reached out to. So, if Dave felt like he was losing control -- for example, if she was giving her attention to someone else, for instance the army - he would become handy with his fists.

She wondered many times about leaving him. But with a baby? There was not a chance in hell that she'd be able to support herself and a child at her rank. And being a single mother in the army, well that was unheard of, unless she put the child in full time nursery, and she took a desk job. That wasn't the life that she wanted for her baby, nor for herself. But his behaviour was escalating, and she didn't know how to stop it. Perhaps Dave had had a difficult upbringing. She'd tried to talk to him about it and what little he had told her made her feel very sorry for him. In her naivety, had she shown him sympathy and excused his behaviour to start with, not viewing it as dangerous?

But of course, it was dangerous. More fool her for not seeing it in the first place. Before she became stuck.

30

It was a wet and windy autumn day, when Dave Cooper finally got in touch with Crane.

The man had done a good job of hiding in plain sight, Crane realised, when the man said he was living in Aldershot.

'Can we meet, Dave?' Crane asked. 'Just to talk about Hazel, try and explore who might have killed her.'

'Not a chance, soldier,' he'd sneered. 'You don't fool me.'

'Fool you?'

'Yes, all you want is to get me in custody and falsely accusing me of Hazel's death. And anyway, I'm wanted by you lot for the doctored protein powder as well. Not that I had anything to do with it, mind,' Cooper finished hastily.

'Dave, I can't arrest you, I'm not civilian police and I'm not even army police, just a consultant helping out with cold cases.'

There was silence on the line.

'Dave? Dave? Can you hear me?' shouted Crane.

But there was no reply. Only a cracking noise. Crane heard someone screaming and another person calling for an ambulance. Finally, someone picked up the receiver and talked to Crane.

'Hello? Hello?' the panicked voice said to Crane.

'Hello! Can you tell me what just happened?' shouted Crane.

'Um, this bloke, he… he was just, I heard a shot, next thing he was on the floor. Blood is everywhere. Someone's called an ambulance.'

'Is he still alive?' Crane demanded.

'Not a chance in hell, it… it… it looks like he's been shot in the head.'

'Where are you?'

'The gardens,' the same said, then the line went dead.

Crane raced over the Jubilee Gardens, near the police station, where Crane found DI Woods who told him that Dave Cooper had indeed been shot in the head and that he had died instantly.

Crane stood there in disbelief. Dave Cooper, dead? Shot in the head? He couldn't believe what he was hearing. All of the emotions he had been feeling about Cooper, anger, frustration, and suspicion, were now replaced with shock and sadness.

He stood there for a moment, taking deep breaths to steady himself. Then Crane walked away. He needed to clear his head and get some fresh air.

As he walked, his mind kept replaying the last conversation he had with Cooper. He had been hesitant about meeting Crane, worried about being falsely accused of her death. Crane had tried to reassure him that he just wanted to talk, to find out what had really happened.

Now, that conversation seemed like a lifetime ago. Crane felt a pang of regret that he hadn't pushed harder to set up that meeting. Maybe he could have helped Cooper in some way, eased his worries, or even prevented his untimely death.

Crane walked aimlessly, lost in his thoughts. He didn't even notice the drizzle that started, soaking his clothes and hair. He didn't care. The only thing on his mind was Cooper's death and what it meant for his investigation.

He knew he had to keep going, to find out the truth about Hazel's death and bring justice for her, incarcerating whoever was responsible. Cooper's death only hardened his resolve.

With a heavy heart, Crane turned and headed back to his office. He would start by reviewing the case files, looking for any clues or connections that might lead to answers. He needed to stay focused, stay vigilant. Because if someone had killed Dave Cooper, they might not be done yet.

As he returned to barracks and sat down at his desk, Crane felt a renewed sense of purpose. He would not let Hazel's, nor Dave Cooper's deaths be in vain. He would find the truth, no matter where it led. And he was determined that whoever was responsible would pay for what they had done.

31

Crane walked to Billy's office and knocked on the window.

Billy glanced up and indicated Crane should come in.

'You alright, Crane?' asked Billy. 'You've got a face like a slapped kipper.'

That appealed to Crane's sense of humour, and he cracked a smile.

'That's better, now what can I do for you.'

Crane had to admit to Billy that Dave Cooper was dead.

'Dead! What the bloody hell happened?'

'Well, I was on the phone to him, trying to get him to talk to me about Hazel's murder, when there was his crack and sounds of someone and something failing and hitting the ground. It turns out that that was Dave Cooper. Someone had shot him in the head.'

'Jesus,' Billy said. 'This beggar's belief.'

'I know,' agreed Crane. 'I went to the site and had a chat with the new DI, Woods his name is. The thinking is that he was killed over a drugs deal that went wrong. But I'm running out of suspects for Hazel's murder. If it wasn't Dave, which seems to be the consensus of opinion, then I've got to suspect Alex Winter, Hazel's first husband.'

'But he's dead too, isn't he? Found dead in that hostel or something you said.'

'Exactly. I'm relying on forensics turning something up. And in the meantime, I'll talk to Cora Young again.'

'Sounds like a plan, Crane. Follow those threads wherever they may go. Keep me posted. And in the meantime, I've my own mess to sort out. Dave Cooper was my lead suspect for the doctored protein powder. Which fucks me right up.'

Crane left the office and hit the phone. He got contact details from Cora Young and talked to Winter's family. His mother and daughter.

He phoned and got them on speaker phone. They were sure that he hadn't killed his ex-wife

'Why aye man, how would he have managed that if he was in Newcastle and she was found in Aldershot?' said his mother. 'He's no driving licence so would have had to go on the train, like.'

'Can you prove that?' Crane said, not at all convinced.

'I've got his bank statements here,' she said.

'You do?' Crane was taken aback. 'Can I see them?'

'I can scan them in and email you them,' said her daughter.

'That would be kind,' said Crane.

'Kind, my arse,' his mother scoffed. 'We want to clear Alex's name. So, give us your contact details.'

The scans came through in 10 minutes and the women were right. There was no debit for a train, plane or coach ticket. So, who the hell killed Alex Winter and now Dave Cooper and why?

32

The next morning, Crane made Billy and Dudley-Jones coffee and asked them to stand around his desk and look at his white board.

It was covered with lots of writing, with arrows between statements and photographs of the suspects. And, of course, a picture of Hazel resplendent in her army uniform.

'While we have coffee, will you help me brainstorm a few ideas about Hazel's killer.'

'Have we anyone in the frame?' asked Dudley-Jones.

'Not really, no. Not since Dave Cooper was killed.'

'Ah yes, you both had him as suspects in your cases,' grinned Dudley-Jones.

Billy grinned also. 'Nice one, thanks for the reminder.'

'Does anyone think Dave Cooper killed Hazel?'

'No,' Billy shook his head. 'Absolutely no forensics tying him to the murder.'

'Not that we've found at any rate,' said Crane.

'What about her ex-husband Alex Winter? The one who died in the hostel.'

'Again, nothing to tie him to the murder.'

'Hasn't there been descriptions of someone lurking around Hazel's house?'

'Yes, Billy,' said Crane. 'But the descriptions are too generic to do anything with.'

'That leaves Arthur Young,' said Dudley-Jones.

'Yes, Hazel's stepbrother.'

'Do we know where he is?' asked Billy.

'Cora Young has given me an address.

'Where is it?'

'Guildford.'

'Best we try and find him there. Have you got any other suggestions Dudley-Jones?'

'No, Sirs, sorry. I'll see if I can do some searches about Arthur Young. I'll let you both have what I find.' And with that he returned to his workstation.

'Am I clutching at straws?' Crane asked.

Billy debated for a few moments. 'Your problem is hard evidence. Forensic evidence. For without that you can't tie Arthur Young to the murder, if indeed it was him. Oh, and don't forget motive.'

'Thank you, Billy, I do know.'

'What was his motivation?'

Crane opened his mouth to answer, then closed it as he really wasn't sure. 'Let's hope we can find him in Guildford and hopefully arrest him. Are you coming?'

'Crane, you can't.'

'Can't what?'

'Make an arrest. You are no longer a serving member of the British Army, nor are you a serving police officer.'

'So?'

'So, the police will have to go with you.'

'To hold my hand?' Crane was indignant.

'Don't be so bloody stupid, Crane. this is just the way it is. You're not being excluded. You'll be there. But we can't have this going wrong because you make an illegal arrest. Remember, you don't have Anderson with you anymore.'

With that Billy went back to his office, leaving Crane feeling that he'd had all the air punched out of him and he was trying to recover. Billy was right, he'd all but forgotten that he needed a serving police officer to make an arrest, being so used to having Anderson with him. Oh well, he guessed he'd just have to find Arthur Young, and then just have a chat. For now, at any rate.

33

Crane spent the rest of that day, hanging around the address he'd been given for Arthur Young.

He also had a photograph of him, which made life easier. The block of flats where they thought he lived, was reminiscent of an American motel crossed with a 1960's concrete block of high-rise flats. There were four floors, with each front door opening onto a walkway. The stairs were on the outside of the building and there was no barrier to entering the complex. You simply walked up to the flat you were going to. No entry system. No closed and locked entrance door. Nothing. Not even a local CCTV camera. Any cameras there were, were, were trained on the parade of shops around the corner.

No one had been in or out of the flat he was watching all day, which was rather discouraging but no matter, Crane had been on enough stakeouts to know that all you did was hang around. He guessed Arthur Young worked. He remembered Cora saying something about him being a mechanic and therefore was pretty much always in work.

As there was still no movement by 4pm, Crane got out of the car and walked around the corner to a local Co-op. There he bought a sandwich and a coffee. He'd been careful to watch his liquid intake, to obviate the need for a piss. He was just leaving the shop after paying for his items, when the door opened and knocked the coffee out of his hand. Hot liquid splashed all over Crane and all over the man who'd barrelled through the door.

'Sorry, mate,' the bloke said.

Crane wanted to growl some expletives at the man, until he realised, he was looking at the face of Arthur Young. 'Oh, no matter,' he forced himself to say. 'But I wouldn't mind another one.'

'What? Oh yes, of course. You go for it. I'll pay for it at the till.'

Arthur Young was as good as his word and paid for a replacement coffee.

As they walked out of the shop together, Crane gave him some blarney about looking for somewhere to live in the area, as he was just about to start a new job. At the same time dabbing at his coat, realising that he'd never get the coffee out, without having it drycleaned.

'Oh, what job's that?' asked Arthur.

'Police.' Crane watched as Arthur did a mis step. But he soon recovered.

'Police? Really?'

'Yeah, I'm a cold case specialist. You know, find the bodies, then find out who killed them, that sort of thing.'

Arthur Young swallowed. 'I'm sure that must be very interesting,' he said. 'Anyways, I really must get on. Nice to meet you mate, and sorry about the coat.'

Crane nodded and raised his cup in gratitude and smiled as he watched Arthur Young rush to his block of flats.

Once at his car, Crane rang Billy. 'I've found him, at the flat that Cora Young told us about.'

'Right, I've already had a word with Guildford and they're letting us use Aldershot police and he can be taken to Aldershot nick for questioning. I'll give them a ring and see you there, in what, about 30 minutes I should think.'

'Thanks, boss and I'll stay here and keep an eye on his front door.'

Billy was as good as his word and 30 minutes later Crane met him and the lads from Aldershot around the corner at the parade of shops Crane had been in earlier.

'All ready?' Bill asked.

Crane nodded and there were grunts of assent from four uniformed officers who'd accompanied Billy from Aldershot. They all moved swiftly around the corner, past Crane's car and into the block of flats, striding up the stairs with ease. Ground floor, all quiet. First floor a couple of kids playing with a ball ran off at seeing the uniforms. Third floor. This was the level. Young lived in Flat 12 at the end of the long open corridor.

They'd already decided not to both with anything as polite as knocking on the door, Billy wanted the door smashed in, and Young on the back foot in surprise.

'Police!'

'Make yourself known.'

'Police!'

'Make yourself known.'

There were only four policemen, but they managed to sound like a full compliment of officers and like a herd of elephants, as they banged through the flat in their boots. Gradually the noise abated. There had been no reply to their shouts. No one had been found hiding around corners, in the bathroom, nor in the bedroom. The flat was empty, even though Crane saw Young enter the flat with his own eyes.

Crane swore in frustration. 'What the fuck? Where the hell did he go? He didn't come out of the front door. I never took my eyes off it.'

'Here, Guv,' someone called.

Crane and Billy went through to the kitchen, to see a back door open onto a fire escape. Crane groaned. How blood stupid of him. He should have checked the back, but that just showed how rusty he was working on his own. He and Anderson had worked so well together that by the end, each of them knew what the other one was thinking, and their movements were almost choreographed.

'How the hell am I supposed to find him now?' Crane grunted, gritting his teeth and working the muscles in his jaw.

'Well, we don't know it is definitely Arthur that we want,' said Billy.

'I know that,' said Crane. 'But he was the best most likely suspect.'

'Ha,' Billy laughed. 'Nice try Crane. Come on, let's get back to Aldershot and I'll buy you a pint.'

34

It was a morose Crane who sat opposite Billy the next morning.

'I've been thinking about what you said yesterday,' said Crane.

'Oh, yes? I said quite a lot if I remember and not all of it repeatable.'

'No, well, sorry about that.' Crane was still ashamed of his lack of due diligence at Young's block of flats. 'But in my defence, I was all on my own. If I'd have checked around the back, I might have missed him going out of the front and visa versa.'

Billy nodded. 'Well, moving on...'

'I think it's DNA that is going to help this investigation,' he told Billy.

His boss seemed to pale, no doubt at the thought of the cost.

'Come on, Billy, I know you're wondering about budget, but let's face it a few DNA tests or traces wouldn't cost much in the grand scheme of things,' Crane urged.

'Which is?'

'It's much less than if I had a team. I'm a one-man band here, as you are well aware, so the cold case department is relatively cheap. Therefore, I'm sure you can pay for a few tests.'

'Oh, all right,' Billy reluctantly agreed. 'But don't go overboard.'

'Who me? Never!' and Crane rapidly left Billy's office before he changed his mind.

He went to the forensics department. 'Bob,' he called. 'My Hazel Cooper case...'

'You mean your only case?'

'Now, now, let's not split hairs,' said Crane and both men

grinned. This was what Crane enjoyed most, the banter between colleagues, all working hard to get justice for the victims they were championing. 'Anyway, you know you'd found unknown DNA on the pillowcase that was around Hazel's head.'

'I do,' confirmed Hunt. 'There was no match in the database. It was thought that maybe if you found Hazel's illusive stepbrother it might be a match to him.'

'Yes, well,' said Crane, 'The hunt for Arthur Young continues. But, could you check the DNA from Hazel Cooper's foetus and analyse DNA from Dave Cooper, to see if he's the father of the child?'

'Yes, I guess. I got a copy of his DNA from Major Martin when he did the autopsy.'

'Well, his death was very clear cut. Shot in the head.'

'By an unknown assailant.'

'That no one's caught yet,' added Crane, meaning Aldershot Police.

'I'll give you a shout after lunch,' said Hunt. 'I'll have checked them by then.'

'Thanks a lot, I'll be at my desk.'

By the time Crane had made coffee, chatted to Dudley-Jones about setting up alerts for Arthur Young, Bob Hunt had come through.

'Here you are, Crane,' he said. 'I thought I'd put you out of your misery.'

Crane grinned. 'They don't match, do they?'

'Nope. Here's the paperwork.'

'Thanks, Bob, it's really appreciated.'

'Anything to get you off my back, Crane,' Hunt shouted good naturedly as he walked away.

I was just as Crane thought. Hazel Cooper's husband wasn't the father of her baby. So, if not him, then who the hell was?

Pulling his laptop close to him, he began to research the glimmer of an idea he had. It wasn't strictly legal, but weighing the balance of probability, he reckoned it was worth the risk.

35

Crane went through the website one more time.

He couldn't do too many tests with Bob Hunt for obvious reasons, but what he could do was pay for DNA comparison himself. He just had to upload a DNA sample. WhoamI?DNA seemed the best overall, from what his research on the internet was indicating. The sequence of events was that you uploaded a DNA sample, and they would match that with DNA stored in their database and then provide you with details of possible family members. That would be great if he was doing it for himself, but of course he wasn't. The plan was to upload the DNA from the pillowcase.

Crane mulled over this for hours. Was he doing the right thing? It was illegal after all, and he was a stickler for the word of law. It was something he lived by. But on the other hand, wasn't it good to have a killer behind bars? That was the right thing to do as well.

And the legality of investigative genealogy, still relatively new, had not faced serious legal challenges. DNA was perceived in law enforcement circles as a vital tool for solving current crimes, and even more so cold cases, but regulations and legislation had not yet caught up with the myriad of options that were now available online to the public and to investigators.

In most DNA-derived cases going to trial, prosecutors contended that the databases police use were like street informants whose identity can remain hidden. Meanwhile, some family tree DNA companies say they have successfully fought off efforts by law enforcement to obtain court orders to access their databases.

However, WhoamI?DNA said on their website that it would work with law enforcement if an investigation involved a violent crime; denying access to data only if a private subscriber to its database has specifically opted out.

He thought that Hazel's killer and father of her baby was likely to be her stepbrother, but he could be mistaken. Crane was convinced he'd find the truth by harnessing genetic technology already in use by millions of consumers to trace their family trees.

And so, Crane finally came to terms with what he was about to do. Instead of swabbing his cheek, he collected genetic material from the pillowcase, which was then sent to WhoamI?DNA, which created a DNA profile and then allowed Crane to set up a fake account to search for matching customers.

Could it be this search that identified the close relative and would help break the case?

36

Crane needed advice and he needed it quickly.

Wanting to keep Billy out of the loop, he made a call and was told he could call round that morning.

Standing on the step, with some trepidation, at the front door of his good friend Padre Symmonds, Crane found himself questioning what the hell he was doing. Was he about to blow his chance at a future with the army? God knows he was enjoying being back, but perhaps he was now taking things too far. He was on the point of running away, when Kim Symmonds opened the door.

'Hello, sir, Frances said you were calling in.'

Crane looked askance.

'Sorry, come in, Tom. Is that better,' she laughed.

'Much better, Kim,' and he kissed her hello on the cheek. Kim had been Crane's office manager when he'd first been appointed to run the SIB on Aldershot Garrison, what felt like many years ago now. After a few years Kim had met and fallen in love with Padre Symmonds, who ran the Garrison Church of England church and had given up her army career when they married. She was now the Padre's office manager and had retrained as a counsellor. She had no earthly reason to continue to call him 'sir'.

Once the three of them were sat in the lounge, with coffees on tables by their sides, Crane talked about his dilemma.

'As you know, I'm looking into the cold case of the bones of a young woman found on the garrison.'

'Francis told me,' Kim said. 'He's arranging a small ceremony for interring her.'

Crane nodded. 'That's right, but my problem at the moment,

is that I can't find who killed her.'

Francis Symmonds frowned. 'That's not like you, Crane.'

Crane shook his head. 'I know, Padre. We originally thought her husband might have killed her, but there's no DNA match to him. We found a pillowcase that had been buried with her. It contains several patches of unknown DNA. That's who I am trying to identify.'

'The theory being that it's most likely the killer's DNA,' said Kim.

'Exactly.'

'And there's no match to your database, nor to the police?'

Crane shook his head. 'No, nothing.'

'Okay,' said Francis. 'So…? There has to be a reason you're here.'

Crane took a deep breath. Then went for it. 'I need some help and advice.'

'Yes?' promoted Kim.

'I uploaded the unknown DNA to WhoamI?DNA.'

'I thought you needed to do a profile when using those DNA tracking sites?' said Kim. 'I've been helping a few clients now with tracing their families using DNA.'

'You do,' agreed Crane.

'And?' prompted Francis. At Crane's silence he said, 'Crane, what have you done?'

'I used my details,' Crane talked to the floor, his arms resting on his open knees.'

'Let me get this straight,' the Padre said. 'You took the DNA from a pillowcase that was buried with our victim. Then you opened an account at WhoamI?DNA using your name and your details. Then you uploaded it all to the website, as if it was your personal DNA. Am I right so far?'

Crane nodded his agreement.

'Let me guess,' continued the Padre. 'You've got a result.'

Crane nodded once more.

Kim put her hand over her mouth. 'My God, you've found the killer! Crane, that's genius.'

'Is it though?' Crane asked.

'Mmm, I'm not sure myself,' said the Padre.

'I don't think it's strictly illegal,' said Crane. 'But morally it must be, surely?'

'Does it matter if the killer is identified?' asked Kim.

'It probably will do if this gets out.'

'You mean you might not be able to use it in court?'

'Exactly,' Crane agreed.

The husband and wife fell silent. Crane once more dipped his head and studied the floor. Then coming to a decision, lifted his head and cried, 'Fuck it. I just don't know what to do, guys. I think it's partly because I work on my own now, instead of part of a team. I don't have anyone to bounce things off. Also don't want to mess up my first case, as I won't be asked to work there anymore. I'm sure of that. Billy is even more of a stickler for doing things the right way, than I am.'

'A stickler for what?' the Padre asked.

'Procedure. He won't deviate from legitimate or legal steps in an investigation.'

'You mean he won't take a chance, or go out on a limb,' said Kim, who knew Billy well. 'You drummed that one into him, sir.' Kim coloured at calling Crane, sir, once more.

'I know I did, but it was only because I didn't want him turning out like me and jeopardising a good career.'

'Like you?'

'A maverick some call me,' Crane grinned. 'I tend to do the exact opposite of what I tell others to do.'

'There must be a way around this,' said Kim. 'Does anyone else know about it?'

Crane thought of Jean Wilder, who he'd told, but she'd promised not to tell anyone. And anyways she wasn't remotely connected to the investigation. Just to him.

'No,' he said forcefully.

'Well don't,' Kim said. 'Just give me a couple of days to come up with a solution. Agreed?'

Both men nodded with alacrity. Once Kim went into office

manager mode, they knew better than to try and interrupt.

37

For 24 hours Kim mulled over the problem.

Breaking it down, Crane had a murder suspect from an illegal (possibly) match on WhoamI?DNA. But he'd done nothing about it. He'd not approached the suspect, nor told the victim's family. The questions was, how to proceed from that point.

Reaching for her laptop, Kim opened the WhoamI?DNA website. She needed to get in touch with the CEO and quickly. She sketched out a scenario and hit the phone. Her request to speak to the CEO was, luckily, taken seriously and it wasn't long before she was speaking to his assistant.

'Good morning, Steve Mason's office.'

'Good morning,' replied Kim. 'I wonder if you could help me, please.'

'Does it have something to do with Mr Mason?'

'Very definitely,' said Kim.

'In that case, my name is Shona. Please tell me what the problem is.'

Kim explained that she was a counsellor, working with the British Army on Aldershot Garrison and also closely connected to the Garrison church. She hoped those credentials would impress and luckily they seemed to.

'How can we help the British Army?' Kim could hear the doubt in the woman's voice.

'I'm involved with a genetic genealogy cold case investigation,' explained Kim. 'And we'd like your permission to upload the possible killer's DNA, to see if anyone on your system is a familial match to our victim.'

'A cold case, you say?'

'Yes, a woman's remains were found on Aldershot Garrison a few weeks ago. It seems she was killed and buried in a shallow grave, approximately three years ago.'

'Oh, how terrible. I remember that case, it was reported in our local paper, as Aldershot isn't that far from Guildford. Look, could you leave it with me, please?'

'Um, this is rather time sensitive,' said Kim.

'Indeed, but Mr Mason returns to the office about 4pm today and I'll raise the matter with him then. Can you give me all your contact details please and I promise we'll be in touch as quickly as we can.'

Kim did as she asked, but as she disconnected the call, she wondered how long it would take for WhoamI?DNA to get back to her. And once they did, what would they have decided?

It was late afternoon and Kim was about to sign out of her laptop, finished for the day, when she got notification of an email. From WhoamI?DNA.

Taking a deep breath to centre herself, she opened the email, to find that the CEO of WhoamI?DNA was prepared to be very cooperative and was happy to work with them in order to generate and search his company's database. The DNA profile would be compared by computer with the profiles of the company's 2 million customers. Kim would be provided with a list of the close matches, including names and other personal information the account holders made disclosable. Steve Mason confirmed that, in his opinion, law enforcement was entitled to go where the public goes. Furthermore, there was a clause that was included in the terms and conditions of the site, that DNA reference samples were given by consent, in order to trace members of their family, wherever and however they may be used.

38

Following Kim's successful foray into the world of WhoamI? DNA, Crane once more went through the steps of uploading the suspect's DNA.

But this time it was uploaded into an account opened for the British Army to use on the site. After 24 hours he got the same results as per the personal account he'd opened.

Right at the top of the list was a man who was a direct familial match to their victim, Hazel Cooper. It looked like he was a close family relative, male, aged 40, living in a small Hampshire village called Long Sutton. His name was Tony Young. A step-cousin of Hazel Cooper, nee Winter, nee Young. Rushing over to Dudley-Jones, Crane got confirmation from him that those details were correct. He explained that it was quite an exclusive village and Crane wondered how Young had managed to buy a house in such an affluent area.

The next day, Crane drove over there and parking his car near the village centre, alongside the pond, settled down to wait for his first sighting of Tony Young.

It wasn't long before Young emerged from his house, which was mostly screened from the road, with a break in the hedging where you entered the grounds. He climbed into a nearly new truck, emblazoned with the name Young's General Builders. That must have been where he got his money from. Building. Or, a more cynical explanation could be that he'd worked on the house in Long Sutton and then married the vulnerable widow.

Crane followed the vehicle to a building site in nearby Odiham.

At the end of the day, Young returned to his house in Long

Sutton.

At that point, Crane also returned home.

The following day, he attended the offices of Aldershot Police, to see the new DI, Lawrence Wood. The man hadn't used Anderson's office, but bagged himself a new, bigger one, at the other end of the incident room.

'Ah, good morning, Crane,' Wood said as he held out his hand and Crane shook it. 'Good to see you. Nice of you to pop in.'

Lawrence sat down behind his desk and Crane looked around. There was nothing there to tell him what the man was like. No photographs. No pictures. No trophies. No child's drawings. Infact the office was devoid of anything remotely personal. Either the man was desperate to keep his home life under wraps, or he didn't have a life outside of work. It would take Crane a while to work out which one was correct.

Undoing the jacket of a suit that looked worth more than Crane's monthly salary, the man enthused bonhomie and Crane immediately disliked him. How one could be so flippant, saying that he was glad Crane had decided to 'pop in'. Blithering idiot. The man knew full well he was coming and why, as Billy had telephoned him yesterday afternoon and arranged the meeting.

Crane handed Wood a file. 'This file details the investigation into the murder of Hazel Cooper.'

'Ah yes, your cold case. Thank you.'

At that point Wood stood, held out his hand once more and said he'd be in touch.'

Crane stayed sitting. 'I don't think you quite understand. How dare you say that you'd be in touch. This is my investigation and I want to be part of the arresting party.'

Wood sat. 'Crane, it was your investigation. Now it's ours. You have no jurisdiction here. I understand Hazel Cooper was in the army, fine. But if you are right about Tony Young being her killer, you can't arrest a civilian. So, as I said, I'll let you know what happens, when it happens.'

Crane stood, fists and jaw clenched. As he couldn't bring himself to say anything polite, he turned and left the prick's office.

Every day Crane rang to speak to DI Wood about the case. Every time he got the message that DI Wood would be in touch. Then Crane had taken to stalking him at the police station, but that didn't bring results either. It seemed that Wood was determined to keep Crane in his place and only contact Crane when he had something to say.

Crane had called into the police station and chatted to the Desk Sergeant, but got nowhere there either. 'Come on, Crane,' he'd said. 'I know you had a position within Aldershot Police curtesy of DI Anderson. But all that's changed now. A new broom has swept through CID. He who shall be obeyed, has spoken.'

It was after 10 long, frustrating days, that Crane got the message that Young had duly been arrested and charged with the murder of Hazel Cooper nee Wilson nee Young. He would be appearing at Aldershot Magistrates that morning. After looking at his watch, Crane ran out of the office, to his car. A mad cap flight through the Garrison resulted in him arriving a mere five minutes before Young was brought before the magistrates.

The man only spoke to acknowledge his name and to plead not guilty. The Magistrate then referred the matter to the Crown Court and Young to prison. Crane looked at the man he'd been chasing for so long. He looked as though he'd been on the run. His hair was longer than in the photographs Crane had seen and the ends were straggly. His skin was dull and sallow and his hands trembled ever so slightly. But it was his eyes that gave him away. Flat. Devoid of emotion. It was almost as though there was no one at home. A killer's eyes. DI Wood reckoned that he had killed Hazel as he, rightly or wrongly, held her responsible for the destruction of his family. Her disappearance had caused carnage within the family unit and he had been determined that she would pay for her transgressions.

It was clear to Crane that they were looking at Hazel's killer. A man who had killed her and her unborn baby without any thought nor hesitation at all.

That night, Crane went for a drink with Billy, Dudley-Jones,

Padre Symmonds and Kim, to celebrate the closing of his first case. He also invited Jean, to introduce her to his team.

'You kept her quiet,' the Padre said to Crane, once she had been given a glass of wine and was talking to Kim.

'Well, it's all very new and I suppose…' Crane didn't quite know how to finish the sentence without becoming emotional.

'I know how strong your love for Tina was. But unfortunately, she's no longer with us and you can't stay on your own forever. She wouldn't have wanted that.'

'No, I know she wouldn't. And I do like Jean.'

'So, give yourself a break and just see where the relationship goes. You don't need to label it. It is what it is, and it will evolve, or not. Anyway, great result in the case.'

'Well, thanks, I guess. But really, I should be thanking you and Kim, for the support you both gave me. I didn't know what to do when I came to see you two. But thank goodness you were able to help.'

'Everyone needs help at one time or another, Crane. The trick is recognising it and acting on it. After all, you weren't breaking the law.'

'No laws weren't broken, but I do think that practices were bent,' Crane said to Jean Wilder later that evening as he recounted the details of the investigation they were celebrating the conclusion of. 'Still, investigation by nature has always tended to include a little bit of deception,' he grinned to lighten the mood. The last thing he wanted was to become maudlin after a couple of pints of cider.

Despite the sticky subject of DNA identification, Crane believed that justice had prevailed. 'The truth is what's important,' he concluded. 'After following leads and piecing together the evidence, the perpetrator had been identified, the charges had been brought, and justice had been served,' he finished with satisfaction and toasted her with his glass.

39

Crane was up in the bedroom getting ready.

Daniel was in the garden with the au pair, putting out toys to play with. As he dressed, he thought of Jean Wilder. He had to admit she was nice to have as a friend. There was no doubt he was attracted to her, but he needed them to be friends first of all. Tina, after all had been his best friend and Jean was fast becoming the same. They were taking their relationship slowly, but he had made the conscious decision to have her in his life. She would meet Daniel today and she was bringing her young granddaughter to play with him.

The satisfactory conclusion to the case had put Crane on a much firmer footing with Billy's investigative team and he was looking forward to his next challenge. Dudley-Jones continued to support him for all things computing and Bob Hunt was willing to prioritise Crane's requests, so they'd go to the top of the queue.

Jean Anderson had celebrated her husband's retirement by booking a cruise. Anderson wasn't altogether sure about it, he'd confessed to Crane, but Jean was determined they would do something together as a couple for once. And this was one holiday that wouldn't be interrupted by his job.

Billy had given the team the good news that Emma was expecting their first child, although there was no such announcement from Padre Symmonds and Kim.

Glancing at his watch, he hurried to finish getting ready. He'd invited them all over for a BBQ, as they were experiencing an Indian Summer and he was looking forward to it, as it would no doubt be the last of the season.

40

Billy had one last thing before he could shut the barracks down for the weekend.

Echoing in his head was the line, 'The soldiers involved in the drugs scandal were gym rats rather than recreational drug users, and they're guilty of being stupid for not checking what was in the fat-stripper product, but that's all.'

With this echoing in his head, he connected to the zoom meeting with Lt Col Carr.

'Right, Williams,' Carr said, 'let's have it.'

The two men discussed the case, the ups and downs of it, the moral position and the legal position. Carr listened to Billy's point of view and the information about Dave Cooper.

After the best part of an hour the decision was made. Carr would dismiss the two sergeants who should have known better and checked the ingredients in the powder they were buying and recommending to their lads. But the 15 gym rats were pardoned, but would suffer a demotion and a dressing down.

As Billy closed the call, he could hear Crane in his head saying that what mattered was finding the truth. Billy had certainly done that and successfully negotiated that at least 15 soldiers wouldn't lose their jobs.

Glancing at his watch, he realised how late it was getting. He better get home to pick up Emma as they were due at Crane's for a BBQ. It was still a revelation to Billy to find Crane not nearly as curmudgeonly as he had been. Understandable under the circumstances. But as Tina had been gone a few years now, it was only right that Crane should open himself up to new relationships. And he and Emma were both looking forward to meeting the mysterious Jean Wilder.

He rang home to say he was on his way.

'I don't know what to wear!' cried Emma. 'Nothing fits anymore.'

'Looks like a shopping trip is in order this weekend,' he laughed.

'Damn right,' she said. 'It's all your fault I'm in this condition so it's only right that you should pay for a whole new wardrobe.'

'A whole new one,' spluttered Billy.

'That's what I said, so get your wallet out, Scrooge!'

Billy cut the call, mentally wincing over the probable destruction of his current account.

HAZEL -THE TRUTH

Hazel was worn down by it all. Dave was being a dick. She'd just found out she was pregnant again. Must have been that moment of madness a couple of months ago. Bastard.

She wanted to go back to work, but Dave wasn't having any of it. She wanted to abort the baby, but he wasn't having any of that either. You'd think she could stand up to him being a soldier and all, but he had this thing he held over her. Pain. Not for herself. But for her daughter. The bastard dangled that over her. All. The. Time.

She was slumped on the sofa with the morning tv on low unable to do anything. It all took too much effort and energy. Then the doorbell rang.

'Bloody hell,' she muttered, clambering off the furniture. She needed to get to the door quickly, before whoever it was rang it again, waking up Tanya who was having her nap.

She flung open the door. 'Yes,' she barked, still annoyed at being disturbed.

'Ah, there you are,' said the voice behind the mask, then he punched her in the face, knocking her to the floor, stepped over her and slammed the door behind him.

Hazel had hit her head on the stairs as she fell and her vision still hadn't cleared, so she had no idea who was in her house. Grabbing a foot, he dragged her into the kitchen, her head bumping along the wooden floor as she went. As her vision cleared, she saw a man all in black, with soft black shoes, all the way up to a dark beanie hat on his head. Hazel couldn't quite see his face, which was turned away from her.

She was dumped unceremoniously onto a kitchen chair and

pushed under the table, pinning her there.

'Hello cousin,' the faceless man said. 'Have you missed me?'

COLD TIMES

Is it possible to have been murdered, five years on from an assault?

But that's what the military police have to decide. The pathologist thinks so, when Owain Dean slips and falls at home, causing a brain injury.

It now up to Crane.

Can he really prove it was murder, or will he be left with egg on his face?

And if it is murder, where the hell is the murderer?

Now available from AMAZON

By Wendy Cartmell

Wendy Cartmell is a bestselling Amazon author, well known for her chilling crime thrillers. These include the Sgt Major Crane mysteries, Crane and Anderson police procedurals, the Emma Harrison mysteries and a cozy mystery series, set in Muddlebay. Further, a psychic detective series has been written, the first of which, Touching the Dead has been followed by six further books in the series. Finally, the haunted series is a collection of ghostly happenings in buildings or objects. Just click the covers to go to the book pages on Amazon.

Sgt Major Crane crime thrillers:

Crane and Anderson crime thrillers:

Emma Harrison mysteries

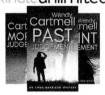

Supernatural suspense

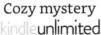

All my books are available to purchase or borrow from Amazon by clicking the covers or entering Amazon HERE. Thank you so much for your support.
Happy reading until next time

Printed in Great Britain
by Amazon